Forever Classics

# RIDE WITH WINGS

*Maryn Langer*

is an imprint of
Guideposts Associates, Inc.
Carmel, NY 10512

A Note from the Author:
*I love to hear from my readers! You may correspond with me by writing:*

        Maryn Langer
        Author Relations
        1415 Lake Drive, S.E.
        Grand Rapids, MI 49506

RIDE WITH WINGS
Copyright © 1987 by Maryn Langer

This Guideposts editions is published by special arrangement with Zondervan Publishing House.

Scripture quotations are taken from the King James Version of the Bible.

All rights reserved. No part of this publication may be reproduced, stored in a retrieval system, or transmitted in any form or by any means—electronic, mechanical, photocopy, recording, or any other—except for brief quotations in printed reviews, without the prior permission of the publisher.

*Edited by Anne Severance*
*Designed by Kim Koning*

*Printed in the United States of America*

Special thanks to the National Pony Express Association and Patrick Hearty, this year's national president, for help in researching this book. Because of them, the names of the stations, tenders, and riders are accurate. Thanks also to the research department of the Burley, Idaho, Bureau of Land Management for making available recent research into the locations and ruins of the Pony stations across Nevada. Librarians in the Western History Special Collection at the University of Utah, the Salt Lake City Public Library Special Collections, the Nevada Historical Society, and the Pony Express Museum in St. Joseph, Missouri, are also among those deserving thanks for research assistance.

## PROLOGUE

The dream woke Braden again—the same dream repeated countless times over the past few years—the dream that always left him in a cold sweat unable to sleep again. He lay in his bedroll under night's lavishly jeweled sky, thinking as he waited for signs of dawn to rise in the western Utah desert.

Always the dream began with Braden riding a borrowed horse, a gray gelding with a black blaze on its forehead. Alone, he and the horse tracked through endless miles of unfamiliar sagebrush-covered hills, snow-tipped mountains dotted high with tall pines that shrank to bunched-up piñon nearer the desert floor, and long barren valleys with only clumps of tall grass and sage to hold the alkali soil. He felt the familiar push of the wind against his wide chest, the hard lash of it across his gaunt cheeks, as he and the horse drove to the top of a steep escarpment. From there, with field glasses he scanned the valley and mountains until he spotted a weathered old cabin. It perched on the wide fan-shaped slope of rocky debris deposited by spring runoff from the mouth of a deep, narrow canyon. *That's a good place,* he would think, not troubled that he had no idea what the shack was to be used for.

Then, shifting his long, lank body until it fit comfortably in the curves of his well-used saddle, he would ride the long distance off the escarpment and across the valley to the lonely windswept cabin.

The place looked uninhabited, but just in case, after watering the gelding at the trough in the corral at the back of the cabin, he would knock on the rough slab door. Almost immediately, on creaking hinges, it would swing open, and there to his startled amazement would be a woman, head bowed, standing in the doorway. Tiny and fine-boned, dressed in a bright calico dress covered with a long white apron, she looked like a favorite doll.

Fixing his eyes on the gleaming hair cascading in golden brown waves to her waist, he watched her raise a tiny long-fingered hand to brush an errant strand back over her shoulder. Then, slowly she lifted her face to meet his stare. Shocked, his mouth gaped open.

Only an oval outline stood out against the hairline. The woman had no face! Her skin glowed flawless and healthy, giving the impression of youth, but all the features had been erased.

She took a step back into the cabin, and with a gentle motion, beckoned him to enter. He stood, rooted to the spot, unable to take his eyes from the featureless oval. Gradually she faded until he looked through her into the black emptiness of the cabin. At this point he always awoke in a cold sweat, gasping for air and shivering.

Tonight the dream had begun the same way, but the ending was different and that disturbed him, disturbed him a great deal. At last, he had seen her face: a fringe of thick golden-tipped lashes framed wide-set green eyes, a small nose pointed neatly at the tip matched her thin angular face. High cheekbones set off the large eyes staring at him, eyes that looked at first glance innocent, untroubled, but in their depths he read hurt and wariness. The full ripe mouth didn't smile, only whispered, "I have been waiting a very long time for you."

"And I for you," he had answered, but when he reached out to enfold her to him, everything, including the cabin, vanished. Braden stood alone on the slope of the empty fan of barren earth, the sharp wind buffeting him, driving its cold deep into his bones, leaving him as always—awake and lost, trembling with the knowledge that in some uncharted desert waited his woman. But, deep in his heart, he also knew he wasn't worthy of her, and because of this, each time he dreamed the dream, he would lose her.

With the first light of dawn, he forced the dream behind him, arose, rolled up his bed, tied it behind the saddle, and swung with practiced ease onto the horse. Braden Russell's face, gaunt, full-browed, wide between the eyes, was set cold and unmoving with his purpose, a purpose that drove him night and day.

He pulled up his fleece-lined coat collar against dawn's chill and signaled the horse, a gray gelding with the black blaze on its forehead. He tried to ignore this horse's close resemblance to the one in his dream. Blast that dream! And once more he buried it deep inside, but he couldn't completely ease the unsettled feeling it always left churning inside.

Braden urged the horse to step away from the dry camp. The gelding moved this morning with a nervousness that gave him pause. Did the animal smell water or trouble?

In the event it was trouble, Braden removed the Spencer rifle from its scabbard attached to the saddle and double-checked the load. Satisfied, he reined the gray to a halt at the crest of a steep escarpment. From this vantage point, Braden let his eyes drift over the valley floor rapidly filling with morning. Silence pooled like water in the basin, even blotting up the ravenous cawing of crows arguing over breakfast.

Off in the distance, a range of mountains chained from north to south, their peaks in mid-February still white-washed with snow, even after the warm thawing wind earlier in the month. Though he had never been here, the country looked disturbingly familiar. He knew without even looking that an unusually deep canyon sliced into one of the distant peaks and from its mouth spewed a giant sloping fan, its flood of debris spread wide across the base of the barren foothills.

Pulling field glasses from a case in his saddlebag, he studied the dark blot on the fan near the mouth of the gorge. The small weathered cabin of his dream! His hands trembled so he could scarcely keep the glasses in focus.

"Just coincidence," he said aloud. "Nothing to this dream business. Nothing at all." *Then why did you pick this particular horse from all those you had to choose from at Buckland's Station?* he asked himself and ignored the answer.

Braden Russell was a determined man, letting nothing stand in his way. He had two purposes in life: find the killers of his sister and set a route for the Pony Express. The thought of the first purpose caused his mouth to tighten into a grim line and his eyes to harden, cold as silvery steel.

But, though the first goal was never far from his mind, he now forced himself to think only of his second purpose, the search for the best route for a new business being started by Waddell, Russell, and Majors out of St. Joseph, Missouri. Already successful overland freighters, they saw a need for fast mail delivery from the East to California. Braden, well-known in the West as a reliable supplier and scout, was approached in January by Bolivar Roberts, the western superintendent, to help set the horseback route across the desert to Salt Lake City. He was also to determine suitable locations for way stations so riders could change mounts and rest.

Braden concluded that if that canyon above the cabin were passable, it would make a fine shortcut for the Pony Express riders. Might even consider using that cabin as a way station if there were water. *You know there's water, Russell, good water.* He pushed back the eerie familiarity of the landscape and edged onto the trail off the escarpment.

This morning, he rode across the valley traveled so frequently in his dream and straight to the cabin. As in the dream, he watered the horse at the trough in the corral, tied the animal to the corral fence, and on legs made unsteady by anticipation and dread mixing inside, forced himself to walk to the door.

As he took several deep breaths, he clasped and unclasped his hands nervously. *Russell,* he thought, *you're carrying on like a crazy man. There's nothing to this dream stuff.*

Braden raised his fist to knock on the door. The thought of the faceless woman caused him to shiver with a cold sweat, and he licked his lips with a tongue suddenly gone dry.

He waited, then rapped sharply again and stepped back. Though he willed the pounding to cease, his heart continued to thud violently against his ribs, beating out the air from his lungs. The weak winter sun shone on his back and cast his shadow over the door. It would fall on her when she opened the creaking slab. Nothing happened. Growing calmer as the rest of his dream failed to materialize, he knocked a third time. Still no answer. He didn't know whether to be disappointed or grateful.

Finally, he lifted the latch and peered into the murky interior. It was a poor cabin, spotlessly clean, but furnished with the most meager of items: a bed against the far wall and a bedroll in one corner, two well-used saddles in another, a small cooking stove against the wall at the end of the room, a crude table covered with a red-checkered cloth, cheery in its newness. Two rawhide chairs were set in place at the table. The one evidence of anything different from dozens of such roughly wrought cabins was the single window, glass replacing the usual translucent oiled paper, curtained with fabric matching the tablecloth.

*A woman lives here. No man would add those touches.* His heart, which had quieted, took up its racing again. Braden stepped back and shut the door. Placing his hands akimbo on his hips, he scanned the alluvial fan, the hills beyond, and then carefully studied the well-trodden path leading up into the canyon. Did he see something moving there? Quickly striding to the horse, he uncased the glasses again and focused them on the figure of a small woman. The sun caught the bright flowers of her calico dress and sent shimmers of gold through the light brown waist-length hair, flowing down her back. His heart leaped, nearly choking him, and continued throbbing hard in his ears.

Apparently she hadn't heard or seen him ride up. This surprised Braden, for he had made no secret of his arrival. Or maybe she knew he was here and fled from a stranger. He fussed with the cinch on the saddle until his pulse returned to normal, then he rode far enough to see up the full length of the canyon. Empty! She had vanished, differently than in the dream, but vanished as completely, nevertheless. Disappointment surged through him as he strained to see into the deep shadows created by the sheer sides boxing in the narrow cut. The canyon, filled with rocky rubble, rose too steeply as it trailed up the mountain. Obviously unsuitable for the Pony route, it wouldn't be necessary to explore further.

Braden refused to admit he couldn't face the rest of his dream. Rather, convincing himself his business here was finished, he turned the gelding north to find and follow the wagon road east across the desert to Salt Lake City.

## CHAPTER 1

### 1860

THREE QUICK SHOTS CRACKED through the steep-sided canyon behind the lone cabin and shattered the twilight stillness of the high desert. Shelby Jackson froze, the large wooden spoon she was using to stir the biscuit dough poised in midair. Papa didn't have a rifle!

She sucked in her breath. Indians? Outlaws? They hadn't ridden past the cabin, or she would have heard them. That meant they had ridden over the chain of mountains behind the cabin and through the winding canyon, notched deep and narrow into the side of one of those peaks.

Shelby's fear-widened eyes darted to the empty pegs over the fireplace mantelpiece. Papa had taken the shotgun with him. Her mind raced as she dropped the spoon back into the dough.

The pistol! Ducking below the only window, she crawled to the corner and reached for the Colt .44 still in its holster on Papa's saddle. Shelby knelt in the shadows, fright stiffening her fingers as she fumbled with the guard strap. Impatiently she jerked the pistol free and spun the cylinder. It was empty!

Quickly she removed it and reached for a saddlebag. She tossed back the flap and jammed her hand inside, hunting for the extra bullet-loaded cylinder Papa always kept ready. Her trembling fingers sifted through crumbs, dust, and sand. Nothing more.

Suddenly the horses and mules in the fenced area in back of the cabin began to screech wildly. She heard a hollow ringing sound as the logs barring the corral entrance were slammed back. Somebody was after the animals!

"Dear God, where is that cylinder?" she prayed aloud as she located the other bag and dumped the contents on the floor. The cylinder thudded onto the dirt and rolled away. Shelby crawled after it, snatched it up, and shoved it into the revolver. She shifted the gun from one hand to the other while she wiped sweaty palms on her once-white apron.

Shrieks and howls accompanied hoofbeats galloping down the barren slope at the mouth of the canyon and around the rude cabin.

"See anyone in the cabin, Dike?" someone bellowed over the confusion

"Nope," came the faint answer.

"I'm gonna throw a few rounds just for good measure."

Bullets smashed into the weathered logs of the cabin walls, and Shelby smothered a scream in her apron.

Still crouched in the corner, Shelby felt the ground shake as horses circled, sending clouds of dust rolling through the open window. It sifted over the biscuit dough and settled on her face. Her tongue spread a grainy film inside her dry mouth as she licked her lips. With flint-hard eyes fixed on the rough slab door, she aimed the gun heart-high.

During the two months she had called this corner of Utah Territory home, Papa had drilled her constantly for just such an emergency. "Aim to kill," he would say. "Savages, white or red, will show you no mercy. Don't show them any. You wait to be a Christian, you'll be dead or worse."

Tight bands of fear constricted Shelby's chest, causing her breath to come in short, quick gasps. Sighting down the quivering barrel increased her terror as she waited for the marauders. Instead, pulsing hooves thundered away, growing fainter as the horse thieves raced off over the rock-strewn ridge and out into the western Utah desert.

Weak and trembling, Shelby collapsed onto the saddle. She shut her eyes and tried to tell herself she was back in St. Joseph, Missouri, sitting on the stoop of her aunt's boarding house, listening with rapt attention to old-timers telling tales of such attacks. Their stories had badly frightened her then, but now she was learning that even their most overdrawn exaggerations had not come close to describing the real thing.

Shelby heard the crackling of the fire before she saw it. Still clutching the pistol, she stared at the window. Smoke billowed through it in dense choking clouds. Flames danced an angry red along the window sill. Tongues of fire greedily ate their way through the chinks between the logs. Heat pulsed in waves against her.

Shelby leaped to her feet and looked frantically about the room. She was surrounded. There was no time to save anything. She had to get out now! Gathering her skirts, she fled as the old weathered wood began exploding, sending firefalls of sparks cascading through the cabin.

Once outside, Shelby stood transfixed, watching her home burn to the ground.

Papa! Clasping the revolver, she raced up the barren sage and piñon-covered fan of rocky debris behind the cabin. Once in the canyon, she hurried along the winding path twisting around the obstacles on the boulder-strewn floor. High rock walls blocked out all but a thin strip of darkening sky. "Papa!" she screamed over and over as she left the main trail and scrambled up the steep path to the mine, a dangerously narrow and treacherous trail blasted from the sheer face of the canyon.

Arriving breathless at the mine entrance, she saw him by the flickering yellow flame of the lantern. Her father lay crumpled in a heap just inside the mine, two arrows piercing his back.

"Papa, what have they done to you?" she cried, becoming cold with dread. She knelt and bent over his body, listening for a heartbeat. "Please, God, don't let him be dead. Please!" she implored. But even as she continued to listen and pray, she knew it was too late.

Shelby stared at his gnarled hands lying still, lifeless. He had spent his life longing for an easy way to a life of luxury. Now, just when it was once again within his grasp, he had lost it permanently.

"Oh, Papa, Papa," she moaned softly before the tears started. "Why? You never hurt a living soul. You only wanted me to have what you never had—security and some hope for the future. Why did this have to happen just as you had really and truly struck it rich, at last?"

The gold! The assayer said it was high grade ore, and he knew people who would pay well for a good mine. He had promised to keep silent until Papa made up his mind. Only yesterday Papa had made the decision to seek a buyer, sell the mine, and go back home to Missouri.

She picked up the lantern and hurried into the little side tunnel where Papa kept the ore. The shadows danced in weird contortions over the walls and empty floor. The gold was gone! They had not only reduced her home to rubble and killed her father, but now all that he had labored to achieve was gone too.

Stunned beyond further thought or action, Shelby sank down beside her father's inert body. Papa had had such plans for taking her away from the housekeeping drudge she had become at Aunt Hally's boarding house. Make her into a lady fit for a gentleman.

Below, the cabin—their cabin—lay in ruin. Fingers of flame still flickered in the darkness, marking where it had once stood—a monument to a dream.

At twenty-two, Shelby had known more than her share of heartache and bitter disappointment. Her mother had died at Shelby's birth, and Papa's sister, Aunt Hally, had taken Shelby in when her distraught father disappeared, returning only infrequently over the years. After each short visit, his talk filled with dreams of becoming wealthy, he would vanish until the next time he seemed on the verge of striking it rich.

Shelby worked for her keep in Aunt Hally's boarding house. When her aunt had died suddenly after Christmas three months ago, her children immediately sold the business. Though Shelby had been urged to stay on by the new owner for as long as she liked, her life began to feel like a prison sentence.

When Papa came East for Aunt Hally's funeral, Shelby, all alone now, begged him to stay awhile, hoping to eventually persuade him to settle down in St. Joseph. As they talked about the gold mine he had found, a spark of hope ignited. He begged her to return west with him, keep house while he dug the gold he knew was there. Then, when he had proved the mine, they could sell it and take the money from the sale and build a beautiful home in St. Joe. he would enter politics, and until Shelby married a suitable man, she would oversee the running of the house and be his hostess. But that was all in the past.

She gave a long shuddering sigh and stared into the tired face of her father, a man made old before his time by years of hard work and harder luck.

Shelby shook her head, attempting to clear it of the dreadful events of the last moments—moments that had again irrevocably changed her life. Numb with grief and fright, she lay curled there on the hard dirt until the damp cold penetrated the thin fabric of her dress. She shivered, wishing for protection against the chill night air of the desert. Then she remembered the blanket Papa used to cover the ore sacks.

Afraid to take the lantern from where Papa lay, lest the coyotes come too close, she groped her way back into the mine to get it. Ignoring the dirty condition, she wrapped it around her shoulders and stepped outside onto the narrow rock ledge jutting above the canyon floor.

Tonight as she rested against the rock of the mountain,

stars undimmed in the clear March air filled the great desert sky. She watched as hundreds of them streaked across the blackness, tracing their deaths in a blaze of light. "A heavenly display to welcome my papa," Shelby whispered through her tears. In her heart, she longed to shout her anguish and her anger against the black velvet sky, but only pitiful whispers escaped the crush of grief filling her chest.

She sat staring blindly out beyond the funnel of the canyon into the shadow-filled desert. From each shadow crept more shadows, each weaker than the last, until there was left only a murky blur on faded stones.

Hours of unthinking numbness passed until at last she forced herself to face her uncertain future. She must try to sort out some plan for her life. Right now, being a young woman was a terrible liability, one that could get her killed if she were discovered alone.

It was a terrible mistake Shelby wasn't born a boy. Papa had even given her a boy's name.

Always under the shadow of Aunt Hally's beautiful and talented daughters, Shelby seemed clumsy at all the things girls were supposed to do well. It was a continual exasperation to Aunt Hally when Shelby's stitches were large and irregular, or she either burned or undercooked the supper. Fearful of what she would break next, Aunt Hally wouldn't let her dust the parlor.

Shelby worked very hard, but she was so tiny the only things she did to suit her aunt were scrub and wash, and hang an orderly wash. Secretly, she kept a miniature zoo of abandoned animals hidden in an old barn on the outskirts of St. Joe. With her work, devoted church attendance, and her animals, she had time for little social life. Instead, she had begun to dream along with Papa that he would strike it rich and be there to take care of her.

Shivering from the black rivers of cold air, she curled deeper into the frayed blanket. Finally, sometime in the early morning, the dam in front of her tears burst, and she wept out her grief in great body-wracking sobs.

Quiet at last, she turned to look at the body of her

father and prayed, "Dear Lord, protect Papa and me. Keep us both safe. Please."

Daylight was creeping into the valley when Shelby opened her eyes and blinked in confusion. Then the happenings of the night engulfed her. Papa was dead—as dead as the empty lantern. Animal prints surrounded them, but they had made it safely through the night.

"Thank you, Lord. Thank you for hearing and answering my prayer, for I am safe and I know Papa is in heaven. I rest in that knowledge. Now please help me face whatever lies ahead."

Shelby stood and stretched her cramped muscles. How was she going to bury her papa? The ground was too rocky for her to dig. Then she knew. Papa had been digging not far from the entrance, and near the shallow hole lay the shovel and pick he had dropped when the robbers surprised him. Papa could be buried right there. How ironic he had dug his own grave. With the back of her hand, Shelby wiped at the blinding tears.

Purposely she made her mind a blank and dragged his thin body to the spot. Then she carefully pulled him in. She removed her apron, laid it over his face, and gently covered him with fine sandy dirt and rocks. Finished, Shelby knelt and wept as she prayed. Loathe to leave her father alone with the animals and Indians, miles away from even the freight wagon route that ran north of the mine, she lingered over the rock-strewn grave.

At last she rose to her feet, squaring her shoulders. It was obvious that she couldn't stay here with no cabin, no food, no money. Suddenly Shelby thought of the horses and mules. She would ride to Salt Lake City and sell the animals. They would surely fetch enough to purchase a ticket on a stage going east.

She ran down the hill to the corral. It was empty! In her shock and grief she had forgotten the animals had been stolen. Wearily she hung over the fence poles, too distraught to move. How long Shelby stood, she did not know, but the sun was well up when she finally came out of her stupor and looked about. She must do something and do it quickly. Remembering Aunt Hally's saying, "The Lord helps those who help themselves," her decision came clearly. She must leave at once.

The mine drew her like a magnet, and she returned with plodding steps. Inside stood a bucket of water. Having located a battered tin cup, Shelby took a long drink, then filled a canteen left lying on the ground. She looked down at her thin leather boots and long full-skirted dress and knew this wasn't fit attire for hiking who-knew-how-many miles. She must devise something more appropriate. Then she remembered the clothes she had worn when she helped her father in the mine.

What had she done with them? After searching, she found them wrapped in a bundle at the back of the shaft. She sighed and changed into the worn work clothes—a buckskin shirt and gray pants that tucked into scuffed knee-high boots. After tying a yellow bandana about her neck, Shelby slipped on well-used gloves that did very little to prevent callouses or broken nails, but would protect against the frigid temperatures of the desert at night. She picked up her father's black slouch hat from the ground, where it had fallen when he was shot. It was so old the black had molded to dark green, and she slapped it against her leg to dislodge some of the dust before she crammed it on her head. Shelby anchored her pants with a leather belt and rolled the tin cup inside the frayed khaki blanket.

Looking down at herself, Shelby took note of her shapeless figure. She had long fretted over the absence of curves, but it occurred to her now that such a lack just might save her life. Along with her target practice, her father had drilled her on the dangers lurking about for a lone woman living in such unsettled country. *Dressed like this,* she thought, *no one would ever suspect!* Unconsciously, she fingered a strand of waist-length hair. Then, it registered. If she were going to pass as a boy, the hair would have to go.

Shelby felt again the prickle of tears but brushed aside the desire to cry. Keeping the hair was hardly worth her life. But where were the scissors? Glancing at the cabin, where wisps of smoke still curled upward to an azure sky, she knew her sewing basket could not have survived that inferno. Then she remembered that she had been darning socks yesterday in the early spring sun. Her father had called her, and she had hurried to the mine, the socks forgotten as he outlined his plan for their departure.

She gathered her blanket and canteen and hurried down to the cabin site. Praise the Lord, the scissors were lying on the chopping block just as she had left them. Reluctantly lifting a handful of gleaming caramel-colored hair, Shelby cut it off just below her ears. The grating sound of the scissors biting off her best feature sent shudders through her, and she clamped her teeth to keep from crying out. Another lock, and another, and the job was finished. She dunked her head into the water barrel and shook her hair, splaying water about like a soaked dog frisking in the sunshine. Afterward, she washed her face and dried it on the bandana.

The sun had reached its zenith before Shelby decided to hike to the freight road. With no money for passage and no hope of getting any, Shelby had no idea what she would do when she arrived.

"Well, Shelby, now isn't the time to fret. First, you must get there." Her low husky voice broke the noon silence and startled a jack rabbit resting under a clump of sage. It hopped away, reminding Shelby how hungry she was and how good rabbit stew tasted. She hadn't eaten since noon yesterday.

"You're wasting time," she scolded herself. She looped the canteen strap over her shoulder, tucked the pistol into the belt, and packed the bedroll under her arm. Shelby slowly passed the rank gray-black heap that had been the cabin. The acrid odor of still warm coals fouled the air and tasted on her lips. After trudging on into the canyon, she paused at the trail that turned up to the mine. While blinking back threatening tears, she whispered, "'Bye, Papa."

Without a backward glance, Shelby set her shoulders against the hard steady climb to the head of the gorge and out over the top. The steep, twisted path was filled with the fresh tracks of horses, tracks made since the big rainstorm ten days ago. Shelby studied them briefly, but they all looked the same to her untrained eye.

She cast a worried glance at the sun setting much too quickly in the late afternoon sky and hurried down the eastern side of the mountain. Once on the desert floor, she kept the hills to her left as she struck out north, toward the wagon road.

## CHAPTER 2

THE WIDE EMPTINESS OF THE BARREN LAND made Shelby feel small, vulnerable, expendable. Nothing but the rush and whistle of raw wind kept her company on this lonesome day. In the clutches of her grief, she longed to be close to someone, to be comforted, to be fussed over, to be loved. But there was no one alive for her in this world and not likely to be.

She sighed, deep and trembling. Whatever became of her was up to her . . . with the Lord's help, of course. Though, with the land so desolate and lonely, it was hard to remember the Lord was also out here.

The wind kept up all afternoon as she paced along the lonely track. The desert crawled ahead of her, straight for the mountains ridged against the northern sky.

Her steps lagged as little by little the shadows lengthened, and she hadn't come to the wagon trail. At last the day dragged itself out, the wind died, and the long shadows of evening stretched across the desert, giving the cold opportunity to settle down again. Shelby blew on her hands and shoved them deeper into the pockets of her tattered jacket. Having no idea how far it was to the road, she dared not think she had missed the man-made road through the desert. If she had, she would be lost in this great trackless wilderness. Full of despair and chilled by the wind bringing in a storm, she realized with increased clarity how frighteningly alone she was. To keep her thoughts from her plight as she plodded on, Shelby prayed for guidance and protection.

Dark began closing over the desert, and she shivered under the rising wind whistling down from the glaciers of the North Country. She must find shelter and that meant climbing into the foothills. Spying a narrow game trail, she followed it until she reached the top of a low rise. Panting, she pulled up the collar of her coat and rubbed the backs of her aching legs. She paused and thought of the steaming hot stew and fresh biscuits—last night's supper burned to a crisp—and her mouth watered. A sharp gust of wind showered her with dust and reminded her to get on with the search for shelter.

Dead grass bent in the steady evening wind. A dozen or so crows raised up as she passed and shouted at her for the disturbance. A great hawk dived to see the commotion, then flew off as if all he wanted was sanctuary from the noise. Dark scraps of clouds blew in and the wind quilted them to the sky overhead. A few scrawny piñon pines stood out, stark splotches against the gray sage-covered mountain. Their dead arms creaking in the wind reminded her of the cruel relentlessness of this barren land.

The peaks above her stood like black sentinels, forbidding, rejecting. Rustlers, renegade Indians, bandits—all manner of threats seemed to be lurking in the ravines and crevices, behind rocks fallen from the cliffs above, and squat piñon, sparce black dots on the hillside.

Her heart began to pound, partially from exertion, but also from the dread of spending another night alone and unprotected. She tried reciting Bible verses, but her mind skittered and slid from phrase to phrase making sense of nothing. So instead she sang "A Poor Wayfaring Man of Grief," forming the words with trembling lips and marching bravely along the foothills.

Shelby had crossed the valley at the base of the mountain and had started toward what looked like a ravine when she heard the sound. Her words drifted to whispers, then faded. She stopped tramping and stood perfectly still, transfixed, straining to listen. Just below the level of the wind she heard it, a heavy lumbering sound punctuated by the grating of rocks and a chinging sound of metal with each step. Something huge and powerful was coming down the game trail from above.

Quickly she crouched and under the protecting darkness, crept off the path into the sagebrush. *Dear Lord, be with me,* she pleaded. As the thing drew closer she held her breath, fighting the fear that was turning her blood icy and making her vision blur.

And then he was standing on the spot where she had left the trail, a giant of a man, enormously tall and coarse-looking, with a long rifle swinging from his hand. In the afterglow before full darkness, streaks of white and red paint showed on his face. But he wasn't Indian. He had blond hair. In spite of willing herself not to, Shelby sucked in her breath and clenched her fists against her lips to push back the scream.

What if he heard her? Saw her? Should she dart out in front of him and race back down the trail? She saw the route in her mind, remembered a fallen log, a large rock, a mound of earth with a large hole in the center, but she was paralyzed with fear.

The giant spoke and terrified her even more. "Ain't nothin' on the trail, Dike. Yer hearin' things in the wind."

Dike! Dike was outside when they burned the cabin! The world spun in a dizzy whirl. These were Papa's killers!

He was joined by a second, much shorter man—his thin body tense, his voice high. "I don't care what you say. I heard singing—woman's singing."

They killed Papa. They'd kill her, too! Only, first they'd do the things Papa had told her about. Trying to make herself even smaller, she curled her body more tightly around her legs and wished she could disappear into the ground. She kept her head down until all she could see were their feet. Encased in heavy boots with

25

thick leather soles and angry-looking spurs attached to the heels, one extraordinarily large pair remained motionless. He had not moved since he first stopped, but remained stationary as though sensing her presence.

The other pair of feet wore soft leather moccasins. Was Dike Indian? The moccasined feet paced in short agitated steps. Leather pants were wrapped tightly around his legs and tied with thongs. With her vision so limited, all her other senses became acutely alert. She was sure she smelled smoke from a campfire, and the rocks clicked together in unnerving little explosions as Dike continued his pacing. She couldn't tell if he, too, carried a gun. Small sharp rocks where she sat bit into her, and the longer she remained motionless the deeper the pain drove. She licked parched lips and tasted the fine powder, bitter with alkali, dusted there by the wind. A bone-rattling shudder convulsed her body. Oh, if they would only go away so she could escape.

"I know I heard a woman singing," Dike repeated. "It was a hymn my mother used to sing."

Shelby shut her eyes tightly, pressed her face into her hands, and bit hard against the rising nausea. These men had killed Papa! A hatred rose, so bitter that it displaced the blood taste, and her whole insides churned with the longing to take their lives in payment for Papa's. She felt the pistol in her belt as it pressed hard against her.

"Not havin' an attack of guilty conscience, are ya', Indian boy?"

The pacing stopped, and the feet faced each other.

"Tell me shooting an old man in the back makes you feel heroic," Dike demanded.

There was a long, ugly pause. "Let's go back," the giant finally growled. "Food's near done, and the rest'll eat without savin' us a peel or bone." The great boots turned, and the attached spurs rasped a tinny clang on the rocks. They walked back up the trail, the spurs chinging with each heavy step. Dike, walking silently in his moccasins, hesitated, shuffled over the area again, then followed.

Shelby's head spun with the conversation she had

overheard. They were responsible for turning her life ugly just when things finally looked like she could have her dreams. Fragmented thoughts of anger, revenge, frustration, and fear ricochetted around her brain, nothing taking full form.

Uncurling her grip on her legs allowed taunt muscles to relax, and the quivering in her legs lessened. At last, when only the low moan of the wind disturbed the silence, Shelby slipped from her hiding place and crept onto the trail. She knew she should flee in the opposite direction from these men, but hate-filled fury drove good sense into the background. She took off her boots and removed the revolver from the belt at her waist. Shelby enjoyed feeling the weight of the gun in her hand as she moved without sound along the dark trail to the edge of a shallow notch in the mountainside.

Dropping to her knees, she crawled to the edge and looked down. The flat bottom was filled with the thaw from winter snow caught by an old beaver pond. The game trail led to this water. Below the pond a herd of horses and burros, hobbled to prevent escape, were grazing on the grass watered by the seep from the dam. Near the water's edge, a circle of men sat around a flickering fire. Each had a tin cup he dipped into the large black pot warming at the edge of the fire.

They kept their hats low over their eyes, and their heads bent over their food. From her vantage point above, she could see none of their faces. However, they conversed in low voices while they ate, and their words carried up to Shelby, listening intently.

"Keep's yer wore out, I'm thinkin', travelin' night and day."

"Cause is just. And the last couple days in the saddle's been real profitable. This here ore's high grade. Assayer said some o' the best he's seen."

"Our cause doesn't make shooting an old man right," Dike's familiar high voice drawled.

"Just how ya' figure yer gonna pay fer a war? With candy drops?" someone asked, sneering.

"Keeping California out of the Union's one thing,"

27

Dike argued. "Killing innocent people for land and property that's rightfully theirs is another."

"Now, now, boys," a big, jovial voice interrupted. "Can't have any fallin' out. We agreed to work together to keep the Pony Express from startin' up. That takes money. We've got us enough in those sacks to keep food and horses, all we'll need, and pay well for information, too."

"I still don't like holding up stages, robbing and killing people. I don't think the good Lord's going to look favorable on a cause that asks that of men," Dike continued.

"Then, may I suggest you ride with me to Salt Lake City, catch the next stage east, and have done with what's botherin' you."

All the heads turned toward Dike. Only a coyote howling far in the distance broke the heavy silence. Slowly, Dike rose to his feet and every head turned. "I need to move around. I'll think seriously about your words." He picked up his cup, turning his back on the men. As he walked silently toward the pond, a single shot rang out. Shelby didn't even see the gun so fast was the draw. Slowly Dike folded onto the ground.

She stifled a half cry, pressing her icy hands hard over her mouth until her teeth cut into her lips, leaving the salty taste of blood.

The atmosphere around changed abruptly, became charged with the ugly emotions of fear, anger, cowardice. Shelby could feel it even where she lay.

"Anyone else dissatisfied with how things are bein' run?" A tinge of venom colored the voice of the man who held the smoking revolver, and the men recoiled from his piercing gaze. He received only an assenting silence as answer to his question.

"Good. Let me know any time one of you feels an urge to change things." Not looking further at the men, with methodical precision he clicked the cartridge and checked each cylinder until he came to the empty one. Reaching into his pocket, he pulled out his loading equipment and began recharging his pistol.

She felt her own revolver, ran her fingers over the polished handle, and sighted down the clean barrel. It would be nothing to kill them and rid the earth of such vermin. These men deserved to die. They were far less than any animal.

Later, after the men were bedded in the circle of light and warmth from the fire, she would creep up and kill them where they lay. Shoot each one carefully, deliberately, and take a full measure of joy in watching him die.

Suddenly, she was oblivious to everything but the deadly hatred filling her. Her mouth twisted into a grim smile as she thought how sweet the revenge—an eye for an eye—was going to be. From her position, she stared into the fire as she waited for the men to prepare their bedrolls. No one went near Dike. There was a wide break in the circle, however, at the point where his body lay sprawled.

They apparently felt secure for they set no guard. Shelby gave grateful thanks. At last the camp was quiet, except for the low moan of the night wind and the occasional yap of coyotes not as far away this time. It was time to make her move. Slowly, she brought the Colt up and set the hammer. There were six men, one for each bullet. She sat up and tried to stand, but the long hours of inactivity and fright had drawn the strength from her legs. She laid the gun across her thighs and massaged the blood back into her calves and feet.

After the prickling and trembling ceased, Shelby grew strangely calm, and a deep cold settled inside. Though she stood, she couldn't take a single step. Her feet seemed planted to the earth where they rested, and her future played before her, scores of vivid ugly details showing her life an unhappy, bitter wreck.

At last, a voice from somewhere outside her said, "We live with what we have created. Love begets love; hate, hate; death, death. Vengeance is mine. Think carefully before you take this step. Once done, you can never turn back."

For many minutes Shelby stood, unmoving as the words reverberated through her. Then, slowly she sank to her knees, bent her head, and felt the tears burn behind closed eyelids. "Thank you, Lord," she whispered. "Thank you for saving me. I will walk with you behind me, in front of me, and on either side of me. I will not fear." Tears washed down her cheeks, carrying with them the hate and desire for revenge.

Looking once more at the repelling scene below, she crept away to find shelter behind a large rock. It offered a shield against the wind, and the old blanket kept out some of the cold. However, she didn't notice. Having been brought to safety from the brink of hell, she slept the sleep of the innocent—warm and deep.

In the morning she waited until the sound of pounding hooves was no longer discernible before moving from her rocky shelter. Then, cautiously she slithered to the edge of the wash and looked in. She recoiled in horror. They had not even buried Dike! Shelby hurried down the trail, found a stick, and in the soft silt scratched out a spot.

Finished at last with the unpleasant task, she sank to her knees on the raw earth beside the shallow grave and bowed her head. "Our Father, who art in heaven, hallowed be thy name. Thy kingdom come. Thy will be done . . ." Her voice faltered. For the second time in two days she was praying over a new grave. "on earth as it is in heaven. Give us our daily bread . . ." The plea for bread was real, and with the final amen, Shelby rose quickly to search for food.

The bandits had cleared away all traces of their camp, and Shelby, though she scoured the area, found nothing, not even tracks. Discouraged and hungry, she collapsed against a rock. Looking at the murky water of the pond, she reached for her canteen, unscrewed the cap, and took a small sip of water as a substitute for breakfast. She tipped her head back and something shiny caught the corner of her eye. While swallowing the water, she carefully replaced the cap on the container of precious liquid, never lifting her eyes from the spot where the object lay.

Quick steps carried her to the clump of willows that hid one of the tin cups she had seen the men eating from last night, Looking over her shoulder, she saw the imprint of Dike's body still visible in the soft ground. As he fell he must have dropped the cup.

Stooping, she found it sitting, still upright and half-full of beans, last night's supper. "Thank you, Dike, for this food," Shelby said as she cradled the precious cup in both dirt-streaked hands, then forgoing manners, gobbled up the contents. Though she was far from satisfied, at least the cold beans removed the edge from her hunger.

For one brief moment longer, she stood by Dike's grave. "I came so close to choosing the wrong path. I let grief cloud my vision, but I'll try never to loose sight of the path again. I wonder where you went wrong, Dike?" Tears again slipped down her dirt-streaked cheeks as she repeated, "He restoreth my soul: he leadeth me in the paths of righteousness for his name's sake. Yea, though I walk through the valley of the shadow of death I will fear no evil: for thou art with me; thy rod and thy staff they comfort me . . ." Shelby continued to repeat the comforting promises of the Twenty-third Psalm as she followed the wash down to the valley floor, then turned north again toward the freight wagon road.

## CHAPTER 3

THE SEARCH FOR THE OLD MULE SKINNER had led Braden Russell down a thousand-mile trail of endless disappointing rumors. Then at last, chance, or Braden's answered prayers, brought them face to face in a Salt Lake City hotel deep in Utah Territory.

Braden, arms resting on the supper table, watched the leather-tough man sitting across from him. He knew the mule skinner only as Will. Here in the West, though, that was enough.

*I've waited a long time for this,* Braden thought, and wondered at his own patience. It hadn't always been thus. That patience, akin to that of a jungle cat stalking its prey, had been forged in the crucible of raw human suffering. This man Will, a stagecoach driver, held the key to the tragedy that had befallen Braden's family. Since the day of their ambush, finding this one eyewitness had been his one consuming passion.

It had been dusk when the stagecoach from Sacramento to Carson City was attacked. Braden's sister had been killed and his father abducted. The old man had been located three days later, wandering in the Sierras, dazed and with no memory of the happening. All the money he had been carrying was gone and his gun, stripped from its holster.

"I wisht I could tell you more," Will said, avoiding Braden's intense gaze, "but there was so little light when the four of 'em hit us . . . an' with their hats pulled low and kerchiefs coverin' their faces, I couldn't even tell if they was white or savage. They knew just what they was lookin' for though. Went right for your old man. Knocked him out first thing. That's when the young girl got into it. Same one hit her, but her head warn't as tough." He glanced at Braden. "Sorry. Ain't much good with gentle words."

"Go on," Braden urged, his voice flat, low, devoid of emotion.

"They fanned through your old man's clothes. Took an envelope and the satchel he was carryin'. Tied his hands behind him and boosted him onto a horse. Galloped off to the west." Will paused and took a sip of coffee.

"Didn't you think that odd?" Braden asked.

"Real odd. 'Specially since we carried a money chest. Didn't even ask about it. Ignored what the rest of the passengers was carryin', too. Just made sure they stayed inside the coach so's they didn't see much and frightened 'em bad so's they wouldn't talk."

His father's having been the only one so treated told Braden the hold-up men knew of the large amount of cash he was carrying from the sale of a herd of prime mustangs in Carson City, their profit for the year. Others in the group had funds and the stagecoach carried a substantial sum in its locked box, but these were left untouched. This convinced Braden there was a conspiracy to take over their ranch, and he had to know who was behind it.

In a voice dulled with grief, Braden asked, "Why haven't I been able to find you?"

Will stared into his coffee cup. "Hold-up fellas give me a tidy sum to make myself scarce. Said they'd kill me if I showed my face in the territory again. I run for a while but that warn't livin'. Decided I'd as leave be dead as not doin' what I wanted."

Braden flipped a coin on the table. "Thanks. See you

in the morning." He shoved his chair back and made his way over to the empty hotel desk where he waited to register. Leaning on the counter, he continued to study Will.

With Braden gone, the waitress approached the older man, coffeepot in hand. "What's wrong with him?" she asked in a brassy voice that carried across the room.

"I dunno," Will lied, glancing at Braden. "Why?"

"Lost his joy for livin'. You can see it in his eyes. They're dead. No spark." She warmed Will's coffee, poured herself a cup, and sat down.

"His face looks normal enough to me." Will snapped his mouth shut, wrapped his gnarled, big-jointed hands around the hot cup, and stared into the steaming brown liquid.

"Oh, he cares right enough. Too much." Undaunted, she went on, "Seen his kind before. Got one thing on his mind—gettin' to the one done him wrong. Turned more'n one good man bad."

The woman's words bit deeply into Braden's conscience, and he turned away. She was saying things he hadn't allowed himself to think about recently. He didn't want to remember how he'd forgotten God these past months. Forgotten that vengeance was the Lord's, not his. And Braden didn't want to be reminded now. Not when he had his first break in weeks. He had to get out of here, away from the sound of her voice and her probing insight.

He whirled the register around, signed it, picked up the key and slipped it into his jacket pocket. The talking stopped, and Braden sensed their attention as he retrieved his satchel, hoisted his saddle over his shoulder, and mounted the steps. The click of his booted heels echoed through the silent lobby, and he felt two pairs of eyes boring into his back until he disappeared from their view at the top of the stairs.

Pausing, Braden checked the number of the key in his hand, then turned left and walked down the long corridor to the room at the end. But his mind was reeling with the scant information he had gleaned from Will, and his own musings. Chill fingers of dawn had searched him out before he drifted off into a fitful sleep.

A pale sun pushed the biting cold of the early March morning over the rugged snow-capped Wasatch Mountains and down into the city. Braden ate an early breakfast, settled his score for the night's lodging, and ambled down to the freight office. He slouched against the white slab wall of the office and awaited the arrival of the freight wagon loaded for points west.

Even hunched into his coat, the firm angular lines of Braden's wide shoulders remained little altered. His gray wide-brimmed hat, pulled far forward, hid the hard square face, blank with indifference, and gray penetrating eyes above high, prominent cheekbones. A Spencer rifle rested within easy reach against the wall next to him.

The rifle was the first thing he grabbed when the heavy canvas-topped wagon rumbled onto Main Street and braked to a stop in front of the station. Silent passengers waiting inside hurried out, and Will gestured toward a rough bench directly behind his seat on the wagon. When everyone was settled, Braden reached inside the office door for his saddle. He lifted it by the horn, looked briefly about the room, and gave a curt nod to the attendant behind the desk. With a tip of his hand, Will indicated where he wanted the saddle. A head taller than the average man, Braden hoisted it easily behind the passenger bench.

Before he climbed up to take his place beside Will, he gave the three passengers a thorough sizing-up. With a sample case between his feet, the one had to be a drummer. All three looked reasonably prosperous, with an air of subdued excitement which told Braden they were probably on their way to the new silver fields around Virginia City. Seemed nearly everyone was going west these days, he mused. These adventurers were more eager than most, though, else they wouldn't have chosen this particular mode of travel. He suspected they would soon wish they had waited and taken the stagecoach. The big Concord coaches were infinitely more comfortable and, in the long run, faster.

Braden wondered how the men planned to get beyond Roberts' Station? They'd probably try to pick up a ride with some other wagon outfit going farther west. He shrugged. While he wasn't completely satisfied with his conclusion, he didn't feel like spending any more time chewing on it now. None of his business anyway.

Braden, though the food and horse supplier of the Pony Express way stations west of Salt Lake City, had volunteered to ride shotgun on his own supply wagon. Will, one of the best drivers in the territory, was unaware of Braden's real position, and Braden hoped to keep it that way. And not without good reason. Festering in his mind right along with the open wound of his sister's death and his father's madness was the knowledge that someone was molesting his wagons which supplied the Pony Express along the western part of the route. That they might also be targeting those hauling out of Salt Lake City had also occurred to him. This would be the time to find out. Aside from the problems they were causing both him and the Pony, Braden had a gut feeling that these acts of thievery were somehow tied to the earlier violence done his family.

Braden felt himself dozing off and yielded to the urge to catch a few winks. Seemed he'd slept only a few minutes when he felt the wagon braking to a halt. He squinted one eye open enough to see they'd reached the first change station. The others got off to stretch and view the scenery. Braden had seen this country from every time of day and in every kind of weather. Right now he wanted sleep. Since no one in his right mind would molest the freight this close to civilization, he continued napping the rest of the morning. The noon meal stop at old Port Rockwell's tempted him, and he unfolded his long lanky body for the first time since leaving Salt Lake.

It was warming up, so he shucked his heavy coat and tied it behind his saddle. Sitting at the table with Will, he found the conversation was amiable enough; the meal, barely tolerable. Still, he felt better for both.

Now they rattled along the road as it went south nearly

to Utah Lake before turning west into the desert. The hours blended together in a long monotonous string. Braden didn't let the jouncing wagon keep him from dozing again, but on the very edge of sleep, he felt the wagon slow and the horses nicker nervously. Even in his stupor, he knew this terrain wasn't steep. There was no reason for the change of pace.

Instantly alert, every muscle tensed, Braden gripped the rifle at his side. He quickly pulled it up and laid it across his lap. The horses pricked their ears forward, listening to the pounding of horses running up ahead around the blind curve.

"What do you think?" Braden asked Will softly.

"Dunno," he answered as he slowed the teams even more. "Ain't had no trouble on this part of the run before Camp Floyd. Too much army. Nobody wants to mess with 'em."

The easterners sat rigid and pale, but they did have the good sense to kept quiet. The drummer, fat jowls trembling, began sweating profusely and nervously wrung his huge hamlike hands. His lips moved as though saying silent prayers.

*A fine lot I'm cast with*, Braden thought with contempt.

They rounded the hairpin turn and were almost run down by a troop of soldiers charging at full gallop. The conversation between Will and Braden halted as the old skinner applied all his skill to keep the teams from bolting.

The officer in charge reined in his horse. "Sorry. Didn't realize you'd have come this far. Been more raiding on the western desert. We're here to provide you escort at least as far as the Deep Creek Station. Farther, if necessary."

"Much obliged," Will said when he had the teams under control.

Braden scowled in frustration. With an armed escort, nobody in his right mind would make a run on the wagons. He would just have to wait for another chance to find out if the gang he was after was operating in these parts. Still, he didn't have the right to endanger wagons belonging to someone else, or the passengers, no matter how insipid, so he kept quiet. Now he was sorry he didn't have a horse to ride home instead of making this slow, bone-jarring trip.

The troops fell in around the wagon, and both the driver and Braden flipped their bandanas over the lower half of their faces. The unprotected passengers choked on the thick alkali dust raised by the horses.

Finally as they neared Camp Floyd, Will exploded. "I ain't gonna ride with this dust all the way to Deep Creek! If those danged savages want this wagon, they kin have it, long as they leave me my scalp!" He looked at Braden. "Besides, a few good shots from that rifle of yourn'll keep anything with sense away."

Rolling up to the station in Fairfield, north across the gully from the army camp, Will pulled down his dust-filled red bandana.

"Loo-ten-ut!" he bellowed and spat a thin shot into the dust.

The young officer who had approached them earlier cut back from the front of the line. "Yes, sir."

"Son, up thar whur the air's clean, this detail ain't so bad. Here in the middle, it ain't fit to breathe. We're takin' it in bits and chewin' our quota. If it's all the same to you, I'd just as soon risk a raid as smotherin' to death. Got me a crack shot ridin' shotgun. I reckon we kin make it through."

"I'll tell the captain. If you don't see us in the morning, you'll know he took pity on you." With a quick salute and a grin, the lieutenant snapped a short command and the military guard galloped off to camp.

Little clouds of dust swirled about each man as he jumped down from the wagon. The passengers were removing handkerchiefs they had finally been wise enough to tie over their faces.

Braden gratefully eyed the familiar building. The hotel wasn't large, but all the walls were made of thick adobe brick. It was quiet inside. Maybe he could get a decent night's sleep if he could pick his room.

Once inside, he said to the clerk, a man he hadn't seen before, "I want a single room. Don't want to share."

The clerk stood unmoving, sizing Braden up. "Maybe I don't have one."

"Find one!" Braden was in no mood to play games, and he wasn't giving the weasel-faced little gouger any money for the favor. Still the man stood coolly staring, making no move toward the board holding the keys.

Not shifting his eyes from the man's face, Braden casually pulled back his jacket and loosened the guard strap on his revolver holster. Letting his right palm run lightly over the handle, Braden held out his left.

At the implication, the clerk paled and pulled a key from under the desk. He laid it carefully in Braden's upturned palm and slid the register around for him to sign. Braden slowly refastened the strap, flipped the key in the air, and walked away. He'd be hanged if he'd give that rascal his name.

The closetlike room tucked off the summer kitchen was sparsely furnished with an an army cot and a chair. That was all right. He had no need of frills.

Braden ducked through the low doorway, removed his hat, and stretched out on the bed. He needed to do some serious thinking. First, his father and sister, now his supply wagons. What did he have that someone wanted so badly? He studied every imaginable angle, but came up with nothing but the ranch in the California Sierras. Beyond being close to the road to the Nevada mines, his ranch was no better than the ones that bordered his.

Braden roused from his ponderings to eat and then returned to his cot. Weeks of pushing himself, with little sleep or food, had caught up with him, and he slept as if drugged.

At the sound of Will's iron fist on the door, Braden jerked himself awake.

"I hired you to ride shotgun!" Will shouted through the thick slab door. "Get your racked-up body out here! You're holdin' us up!"

Sheepishly Braden sat up and stared at the daylight

framed by the little square window. Shaking his head to clear away the fog, he struggled to his feet, then threw back the latch, and staggered into the kitchen.

"Throw some cold water on your face. Breakfast's waitin'," Will said and stalked into the dining room.

Braden scarcely remembered anything about the next little while. He only knew that when he settled onto the wagon seat, his stomach was full and he was still craving sleep.

"You can keep dozin'," Will said. "Still close enough to the army to scare off any raids."

Nodding his thanks, Braden slanted his hat over his eyes and napped.

The next three days passed in much the same fashion, with the exception of their accommodations. One night the travelers bunked at a Pony Express station, along with employees of the Pony. But with no hotels along this lonely stretch, they curled up near the fire, sleeping under the wagon on bedrolls stretched on the ground.

On the fourth day, they drove along the base of the Deep Creek Mountains. Tonight they'd be at the home station. Since this was where Pony riders slept, Braden could count on a bed. He drowsed on, thinking of that luxury when Will suddenly hollered, "Whoa!" and pulled the teams to an abrupt halt.

"What in tarnation you doin' out here alone, a million miles from nowhere?" Will bawled at the slight figure standing beside the road.

Braden, fully awake, studied the slender youth, no more than fourteen or fifteen years of age. He was pleading with the driver to take him on.

"Please, mister, I'll work to pay for my ticket. I ha— ain't got no money. Please take me."

There was an underlying ring of desperation in the soft husky voice, but Will shook his head. "Sorry, kid. Cain't do it. How do I know you ain't a runaway? Then I'd have your folks on me pronto. Had a coupla kids of my own. I'da shot the man who helped 'em take off."

Something about this boy didn't suggest a runaway, Braden decided. Sorrow was etched on the beardless face and in the cool green eyes. And now the finely cut square chin began to tremble, and something close to panic issued from the stricken face.

Something about the kid's face struck a chord deep inside, Braden shoved his hat to the back of his head and slowly pushed himself to a sitting position. "My money any good?" he asked Will quietly, then wondered why he'd made such an offer.

"You want to be responsible for helpin' a young'un run away, that's your business, I reckon." Will cast an acid look at Braden.

"I'll risk it," Braden said. "Come on, kid. Throw that blanket roll in the back next to my saddle and climb in."

The boy hesitated, measured the distance with his eyes, and gave the roll a toss. Braden watched it hit about where his saddle lay. A tiny smile of satisfaction creased the thin pale face as the youth dusted off his hands on his pants.

Braden held out a hand and the kid grabbed it, boosting himself up to the wagon seat. The men on the bench squeezed together and the boy slid in next to them.

"Thanks, mister," he said softly to Braden, and a small smile hovered at the corners of his mouth.

*When his voice changes,* Braden thought, *he's going to have a bass that'll challenge the best. Hope he grows some to go with the voice, though. Awful small right now.* Braden turned and gave the boy another searching look. *Sure has a sad-looking face for a little guy.*

Will clicked the team into action and the wagon began to move again.

"What's your name?" Braden asked.

"Jackson. Shelby Jackson, sir."

"Where you headed?"

"I guess wherever it is you're goin', since I'm beholden to you."

"Not running away?"

Shelby paused, and Braden watched his eyes sweep over the other passengers. A look of discomfort colored his face. "No sir. Leastways, not like the driver thinks."

Braden grunted and settled back into his seat. *Boy's*

*right not to trust these tinhorns*. The two of them could talk in private when the wagon stopped at Deep Creek for the night.

The Colt tucked in Shelby's belt intrigued Braden. He turned around and said, "Pretty fancy weapon for a kid your age. Know how to use it?"

"I'm good at tin cans and bottles." The boy grinned, showing white even teeth. "Don't know how I'd do in a pinch."

"Hope we don't have to find out." Braden sank down into his seat, and pulled his hat over his eyes, shutting out the sun and signaling the end of the conversation.

The drummer cleared his throat. "My name's Elwood P. Hawker," he said. "You got any folks?" he asked.

Braden squinted one eye open and looked back. The kid's face paled slightly and went blank.

"No," was all he said. Then, glancing at Braden, he too pulled his old greenish-black hat over his eyes and shut out the world.

Braden grinned. He liked the kid. Bet in a pinch Shelby Jackson would come through with that Colt.

## CHAPTER 4

IT WAS DARK when the wagon pulled into Deep Creek Station. Every muscle in Shelby's body ached. Riding a freight wagon over that road came close to a new kind of torture.

Numb in mind and cramped in body, she allowed the kind stranger to almost lift her from the wagon and lead her into the station. He handed her a bowl of something deliciously hot, and after wolfing it down, she allowed herself to be guided to a cot. That was all she remembered until rough hands began shaking her awake.

"Come on, kid," a coarse voice growled. "You want to trail with us, you better get a move on."

Warily she opened an eye and looked into the red face of Elwood P. Hawker, the fat man from the wagon. She sat up and pulled away from his pawing hands.

"Tha—thanks," she stammered and caught herself before she clutched the blanket in front of her. It was hard to keep in mind she was supposed to be a boy.

"Hey, Hawker, leave the kid alone and mind your own business," her benefactor called.

Elwood Hawker turned an even deeper red, swore under his breath, and stalked outside.

"Better roust out now. Wash your face and have some

breakfast. It'll be awhile before you have food this good again."

Shelby liked his voice. It wasn't loud, but there was an authority in it that commanded attention. "Yes, sir," she said and crawled from under the warm blanket.

"Enjoy the luxury of washing your face, too. Don't know where you're from, but in this country water's at a premium. Along the Pony line, there are stations where water has to be hauled in. They won't take kindly to your washing in it." He poured some for her into a basin.

Shelby, trying to remember how boys splashed and made funny blowing noises, dashed cold water in her face. She wished she'd paid closer attention to how her cousins washed. Still, little things continued to occur to her. If she kept alert, perhaps she could maintain her disguise.

"Jackson!"

The sharp tone cut through her thoughts and she jumped.

"Just like a kid," he said. "Stand around daydreaming while his food gets cold."

Quickly she hung up the towel and slid into the seat next to her rescuer. He saw to it that the food was passed to her and soon her plate was heaped with fried potatoes, steak, and eggs. She wondered how she was going to eat it all.

Will looked at her carefully. "Don't know how you stay so scrawny, eatin' like that."

"Don't get to eat like this much," Shelby answered as best she could, her mouth crammed with food. She remembered Aunt Hally constantly yelling at her boys for talking with their mouths full.

Elwood Hawker cleared his throat, a sure sign he was about to speak.

Will interrupted. "If you're goin' to say somethin' to the young feller, don't. We'll never get gone if we have to wait for him to eat *and* talk."

Shelby sent a grateful glance in Will's direction. Something about the drummer frightened her, and she wanted as little to do with him as possible.

Setting down his empty coffee cup, Will said, "All right boys, let's get the stuff off the wagon so's we'll be ready to move out when these late-risers finish their grub."

The crew from the station and the three passengers pushed back their chairs and followed him out into the frosty morning. Shelby ducked her head, eating as fast as she could.

"Don't let old Will rush you," the kind man spoke in a conspiratorial tone. "He thinks the world revolves around him and his schedule."

She looked up into his soft gray eyes, laugh lines played at the corners. The rest of the face remained expressionless. It gave her an eerie feeling. If you couldn't see his eyes, you'd never know what he was thinking.

"Name's Braden Russell," he said casually.

She nodded and continued to eat, trying to be as messy as possible.

Braden sat drinking his coffee and watching her. "Been some time since you were around womenfolk, hasn't it?" he observed drly.

Surprised, she stopped eating and looked up. "Why?" she managed through a mouth stuffed with fried potatoes.

"It's been a few years, but I seem to recall my mother railing at me for stuffing my mouth too full, not taking time to chew properly, and trying to talk with cheeks poking out like a squirrel's. Seems like no one's nagged at you for a while."

She blushed. Maybe she was overdoing the bad manners. It was a relief to be able to slow down and eat like a civilized person.

"More coffee?" Braden asked, coffeepot in hand.

Deliberately not answering until she had chewed every last morsel and carefully wiped her mouth on the back of her hand, she left him holding the black container as he waited. "Yes, please," she said at last, holding up her mug.

He ignored her exaggerated manners, calmly filled the

mug, and warmed his own before setting the pot down. Lifting her hand from the table, he examined it carefully. Her heart stopped. It looked too frail to be a boy's, but two of the fingernails were broken and there was a healthy bit of dirt under all of them and more ground into the knuckles—dirt acquired when she buried Papa and Dike.

"Not very big, but I'm glad to see you've developed some callouses," he commented. "Might come in handy." He dropped her hand and studied her carefully.

She kept her head down and hoped the beating of her heart wasn't visible. If Braden discovered she wasn't a "he," she didn't know what he might do.

"Want to tell me what you were doing out in the middle of nowhere yesterday?"

She really didn't, but having rescued her, the man did deserve some sort of explanation.

"My pa got shot by a bunch on horseback. They burned our cabin. Stole the gold and horses." She shrugged her shoulders, trying to buy time to bury the memory deep enough so she wouldn't cry. "Couldn't do nothin' else but leave."

He didn't say anything for a while. Finally he cleared his throat. "Got no ma, I take it."

She shook her head.

"When did all this happen?"

"Two days ago." It didn't seem possible it was such a short time ago.

A frown flickered over his face. "Don't happen to know who it might have been, do you?"

His voice held an urgency that hadn't been there before, and she found herself telling him the details.

"Did you notice anything unusual about the prints at the head of the canyon?"

She gave him a blank look. "What should I have noticed?"

He started to speak, then changed his mind and shook his head. He sat hunched in silence, cradling the coffee mug in his hands.

She felt terrible. She had obviously failed to observe

something he badly wanted to know. Something that might lead to Papa's killers.

Will banged open the door and shouted, "If you two've finished yore eatin' an' palaverin', we'd like to be off sometime today!"

Shelby gulped the last of her coffee and grabbed her gun and hat.

"Glad to see you didn't forget your revolver," Braden said as he buckled on his holster and reached for his rifle.

She gave him a thin smile and lengthened her stride as she went out the door. The three men sitting on the bench made no room for her. She cast helpless eyes at Braden.

"Will, I think the kid had better sit up front with us. What say?"

"Won't be no problem today. Got some new mules. I'm gonna be ridin' wheel. Be plenty of room on the seat. Less o'course, you plan on makin' it into a bed and layin' prone all day." His wide tobacco-stained grin took any sting out of the words.

"Listen, you old cuss, just watch your mouth. Remember, you're in front of our guns," Braden shot back. He propped his rifle against the wagon wheel, grabbed Shelby's arm, and boosted her into the wagon by the seat of her pants.

She gasped at the placement of his hand and barely caught herself before protesting. Braden swung up easily and stood contemplating the hard board that served as the seat.

"Sure would be easier to endure with a little padding," he said. "What about that old blanket of yours? Mind if we sit on it?"

Willingly she climbed into the back and retrieved it. They spread the dilapidated blanket over the seat while Will watched them, a sour look fixed on his weathered face.

"If your royal highnesses is finished upholsterin' your seat, I'd like to be on our way."

Braden gave a wide sweep of his hand and the first sign of a smile that Shelby had seen. "Move 'em out."

The days passed in monotonous succession. Braden and Shelby jounced and jarred through the desert during the day and bedded down at night in front of the fire or in one of the Pony Express stations.

Conversation dwindled to the briefest of exchanges. Even the bragging ceased, and a glazed look replaced that of excitement and expectancy. Elwood Hawker lost weight and his jowls sagged, giving him a bulldog appearance. He looked utterly miserable.

"Don't know why I let you fellers talk me into this shortcut," he whined to the other two men. "Shoulda known better, being on the road as many years as I have. No such thing as a shortcut. You either pay in money or in personal agony."

Just then, the wagon, which was crawling up another mountain pass, hit a hole in the road. At the ensuing bounce and jerk, there were particularly loud pitiful moans from the rear.

"You fat slob, stay on your side of the bench or I'm pitching you out the next time," one of the passengers growled.

"Yeah, you and who else?" Elwood Hawker retorted, bristling under the threat.

"Me," the smallest man said with a suggestion of quiet menace.

And so they bickered like spoiled children until Braden had had enough. He slowly straightened in his seat, pushed his hat to the back of his head with his thumb, and turned a beard-shadowed face to the men. With elaborate motions, he unstrapped the Colt from its holster, and drew a bead on the drummer.

Shelby's fingers tightened into fists. Was this kind man really going to shoot? she thought frantically. The looks on the faces of the men said they thought he was.

"Gentlemen," Braden said in a steely voice, "I have been duly commissioned to remove, by any means I deem appropriate, any obstacles hindering the progress of this wagon. I hereby give notice that the three of you are 'obstacles.' Is there any question about how I shall remove you?"

Three heads, eyes bulging, moved from left to right in unison.

"Good." Braden returned the revolver to its holster and settled down again.

After this, the only sounds issuing from behind were groans and grunts as they bounced along. Shelby had to admit, as they unloaded supplies for each station and the wagon grew lighter, that the jolting and jouncing increased. But she would have died before making a sound.

Braden seemed to be making the trip without great discomfort, and she watched his body for some clue as to his secret. He rode the wagon as one would ride a horse, relaxed and in rhythm with the movement. She tried relaxing too, but concluded nothing was going to turn this freight wagon into a Concord stagecoach. Will had the smartest solution, she decided. Riding the wheel mule couldn't possibly be as wearing as riding in the wagon. Her drowsy meanderings were suddenly interrupted.

"Hold on!" Will shouted as the wagon lurched through a recently washed gully.

The accompanying jolt sent Shelby flying into the air. She grabbed frantically for the arm rest and missed. She was in free-flight like the first time she had been thrown from a horse. The flying was fine, but she clenched her teeth in anticipation of the landing.

Then a strong hand grasped her arm and dug in, pulling her back into the wagon. Instinctively she turned into the sheltering shoulder and found Braden beside her. Despite her best efforts, she shook uncontrollably and couldn't find her voice.

He patted her roughly on the shoulder. "Take it easy, kid. You're fine."

The wagon gave another violent lurch and they clung to each other in an effort to stay upright. The sound of splintering wood rent the air. The passenger bench split, depositing the men on the floor of the wagon. In spite of Braden's warning to them, they let out frantic yells and curses.

"Will!" Braden shouted. "Stop this contraption before you kill us all!"

Will turned a sleepy face to the irate group. "Sorry," he muttered and reined the mule teams to a halt. "Guess I dozed off a spell."

In those brief seconds in Braden's arms, Shelby had felt the steel-corded muscles of his back and drew a comfort she had never felt before. Shelby liked being held by him. Liked it a lot.

At the same moment, he thrust her back, looked down into her face, and shoved her onto the seat.

"Hang on," he ordered brusquely and withdrew as far from her as the seat allowed.

"What'll we sit on?" Elwood Hawker demanded of Will.

"There's some sacks of beans under the canvas. Pull up two or three. Just watch you don't bounce on 'em too hard and split 'em."

"Why, you miserable old cuss," the drummer sputtered, "watch where you drive this wagon and you won't have to worry about what we do to your bean sacks."

The disgruntled men started to throw away what was left of the seat.

"Hang on to that wood," Will ordered. "We'll use it for fires along the road."

They dragged up the sacks and stacked them against the wagon box, using the sides as a backrest.

When the men were seated, Will cursed the teams back into action, and Shelby turned her head away, struggling to get her emotions under control. *Shelby, you know absolutely nothing about Braden Russell. You're frightened and alone, and he's the only one who's offered you any kindness. Try to remember you're a boy, will you, and stay out of his arms!*

Braden pulled his hat low over his eyes and stared unseeing out into the desert. What was the matter with him? The feelings that shot through him when the kid was in his arms were not at all what he should be feeling. He sat chewing on his thumbnail, trying to understand what had just happened. Maybe this was the way it felt to be a father. Since he had never even been close to becoming one, he didn't know. After he thought about it some more, he decided that must be it. The feeling of wanting to protect and touch. Sure! He remembered when his father had put a loving arm around his shoulder. A couple of times when something went really bad, he had put both arms around Braden and pulled him to his chest.

But it beat him why he felt all quivery when he looked into those liquid green eyes framed by long thick lashes. Eyes bright with unshed tears. And the sensitive mouth. The full lips. Lips that quivered in fright. Braden's fingers still remembered the feel of the soft hair when he pulled the small head against him.

He shifted slightly in his seat and glanced at the kid hunched against the arm rest, gripping it until his knuckles went white. Braden desperately wanted to reassure the poor orphan, tell him not to worry. Tell him that he'd be taken care of, no matter what.

## CHAPTER 5

BECAUSE OF THE UNSEASONABLY heavy blizzards, the supply wagon didn't arrive at Roberts' Creek Station until late March. Shelby had had much time to ponder the death of her father. She longed to know who killed him and why. She still had the mine, and the gold had been scarcely touched, according to Papa. But without money, who could she get to work for her? Who could she trust? Maybe the killers would come back and take the mine, too. Maybe they already had.

"You planning to stay in the wagon and go back to Salt Lake City?"

Braden's question interrupted her thoughts. She blinked out of her trance and looked at the crude log cabin. Will had unhitched the three teams, and a stranger was leading them into the corral attached to the station. Shelby sat clutching the blanket around her.

"Is this really Roberts' Creek Station?"

"Disappointed?" Braden asked, reaching up a steadying hand to help her from the wagon.

"From the way everyone talked, I expected somethin' a lot bigger," she answered. "Seems pretty puny to me."

"Don't look so dejected, kid. It's not the end of the

world." Braden threw a careless arm around her shoulders and propelled her blanket-wrapped body toward the cabin.

A terrible urge swept over her to cuddle close into the protection his arm offered. She ducked away from him lest she succumb to the temptation. "Maybe it's not the end of *your* world, but mine looks awful hopeless right now."

They stomped into the shelter of the log walls and out of the fierce biting wind. After introductions and sleeping arrangements were made, Braden continued the conversation.

"What's the big problem?" he asked, hunkering down in front of the fire and handing her a mug of steaming coffee.

Shelby wrapped chilled hands around the mug and curled up beside him. "I don't have no money, no idea how to get some, and I'm beholden to you," she said.

"Don't worry about it. We'll settle up later."

"How?"

"Your prospects are better than you think. I've had my eye on you. I think you'd make a good stablehand for the Pony Express."

"Here?" Shelby gasped and her eyes widened in shock. She gulped and wished she could recall her words. But in her present circumstances, she had no right to act uppity. She should hope and pray they would hire her anywhere on the line.

"Oh, I don't know. It was just a thought." Braden stood abruptly, leaving her alone to meditate on her hasty reply.

Supper over and dishes cleared away, the men took out their pipes, and Elwood Hawker produced a deck of cards. They all gathered around the table. "Come on, kid. Pull up a stool and join us for a little game," he urged Shelby.

"Uh, I'm not much good at cards," she stalled. *That was an understatement,* she thought. Why, she'd never played cards in her life! "Besides, I ain't got no money."

"By the way, Pete," Braden said to Pete Neece, the

station tender, "you look short-handed. Got a place for the kid here as a hostler?"

"Like to give him a job so's I could beat the pay out of him at cards, but I'm full up right now. These two fellers you brought down from Salt Lake City decided to stay and help me out."

Shelby watched Braden's face, but there was nothing in his expression to reveal his thoughts. Still he had to be surprised at the news. If he'd known their plans, he wouldn't have asked about a job for her. Funny, they didn't look like men who'd want or need this kind of work. Didn't seem planned, either. Their talk had been only of Virginia City and the silver mines.

Spreading her blanket by the fire, Shelby curled up and stared into the dancing flames. She couldn't stay here, but where could she go with no horse and no money to pay passage back with Will? *Dear Father in Heaven, I bring my heavy burdens to you. I know you will show me the way. Please give me the faith to follow.*

"Figure this weather'll stop the first Pony run next week?" Pete Neece asked.

"If it does, then the Pony'll never run again," Braden observed.

Elwood Hawker coughed. "I hear rumors the weather's not the only thing against the Pony. Indians aren't too happy with their treatment from the miners. Some are talkin' war."

The arrows in Papa's back flashed into Shelby's mind. Had the war already started? If so, perhaps she was the only one who knew.

The game went on and in the drone of the men's voices, Shelby, worn from days of unceasing frigid wind and battering by the wagon, lost consciousness.

She was aroused in the morning by the groans of disgruntled men and the shuffle of feet as they stepped over and around her.

"Come on, kid, get outta the way!" Pete Neece urged.

Shelby flipped over and crawled away from the fireplace. She was barely quick enough to miss being smacked by an armload of logs Pete began stacking on the still hot coals.

Finished, he thrust a bucket at her and ordered, "Fetch some water from the crick and try washin' your face. You're a mess."

*That's not all that needs washing.* Shelby yearned for the luxury of a bath and clean clothes. The ones she was wearing could almost stand alone.

She grabbed the bucket and raced out the door. Once outside, she stopped cold and looked around. She had no idea where the "crick" was. She edged around the corral of snorting horses and mules and scanned the dry gray sagebrush flat. There was a willow-bordered gully she guessed to be a creek bed. She streaked for the water.

Galloping back, washed and panting, she swung open the door, managed to hit the bucket against her leg, and sent a wave of water splashing over the floor.

"If you ain't the clumsiest kid I ever seen," Pete snorted.

"Been so long since you were fifteen, you can't remember you had two left feet," Braden retorted in her defense.

"I warn't never *that* ungraceful. Boy's a menace," Pete growled.

After breakfast, Shelby offered to help clean up.

"No thanks!" Pete snapped. "Them tin cups and plates got to last awhile. You'd probably bend 'em past usin'." He turned his back, stacked the dirty dishes in cold water and set the pan to heat on the small cookstove.

Shelby stood watching as he worked, her thumbs cocked in her pants pockets. She tried standing awkwardly and disjointedly and hoped she looked as clumsy and mawkish as she felt.

Braden ran his fingers through thick dark curls and clamped his hat down. "Come on, kid, let's find you and me a couple of mustangs and get out of here. It's obvious we're not real welcome." He sent a piercing glare in Neece's direction.

After imitating Braden's hair-combing technique, Shelby squashed her old black hat down tight against the wind. She'd lost a button off the old coat and it gaped in the middle. If she hadn't been so afraid of Pete, she'd have cut off the lowest button and asked for needle and thread to sew it to the gap.

Braden nodded and she followed him out into the chilling wind. "Know much about horses?" he asked.

"Not a lot. I ain't seen any that look like these afore," she said as she inspected the deep-barreled, strong-legged little animals.

"These are mustangs from the high rancheros in California. Came from the purebred Arabians left by the Spanish. Stout-hearted beasts, but they kick, bite, squeal, and buck worse than anything alive."

Shelby paled at the thought of riding one of the wild creatures. Papa had insisted she learn to ride astride and she had practiced diligently. But her horse had been an even-tempered, well-trained mare that responded neatly to all Shelby's commands.

Braden grabbed his saddle from the back of the wagon and threw it on the fence. He untied the rope and lassoed a mustang. While one of the new stock tenders held it steady, Braden cinched on his saddle. He did battle with the bridle, but finally had it strapped in place and the horse tied to the fence.

Pete Neece came strolling up about that time. Braden looked over at him. "Got anything a bit tamer for the kid?"

Pete stretched his neck to peer over the milling horses. "Try that little mare there in the corner," he suggested.

Taking his rope, Braden went after the little chestnut mare. She let him cut her out, put the rope around her neck, and bring her to the fence. After examining her thoroughly, he asked, "How about a saddle and bridle?"

Pete frowned. "I know you work for the Pony, but the kid don't."

"You expect him to ride all the way to Carson City bareback?"

"I don't expect him to do nothin'. I don't think I owe him tack, neither."

"Kid's going to work for the Pony farther west. They'll fix him up. I'll send your stuff back on my first supply wagon that comes this far."

Grudgingly Pete went back inside and brought out a saddle and bridle.

"Look, you old skinflint," Braden protested upon seeing the tack, "I didn't expect the best saddle in the place, but I do want more than a bare saddletree with no leather covering it!"

Pete held up the naked saddle, with only dangling stirrups and a cinch laced to it. Its freshly carved pine gleamed a cream color in the overcast morning. "Don't look like much, but it's all I got. A kid named Cates designed the thing. Weighs in at just thirteen pounds."

Braden walking over, lifted the saddle out of Pete's hands, and hefted it. "Light enough, all right, but I'd hate to ride that piece of wood without some sort of covering."

"It's got a leather cover. Called a mochila."

Shelby examined the two large pieces of leather stitched together with strong leather string. There were openings to allow the saddle horn and the cantle to secure the cover in place. "What are these for?" she asked, fingering four leather-covered rectangular boxes, one on each corner of the mochila.

"Holds the mail. Front left is the 'way pocket.' Use it for the mail picked up and delivered along the route. All the pockets but that one are locked permanent at the beginnin' of the trip, either in St. Joe, or in San Francisco. Only home station tenders have a key to the way pocket."

"Boys just shift the mochila from horse to horse?"

"Right. And the mail along with it."

"Well, Shelby's going to break this one in for you," Braden said as he handed it to her along with the saddle and bridle.

Pete's face grew sour as green apples as he watched her spread the protective saddle blanket and throw the light saddle into place. *Thank you, Papa, for teaching me to saddle a horse.*

Pete turned and stomped back into the station. Shelby felt a knot form in the pit of her stomach. She hadn't intended to make Pete angry, but it seemed nothing she could do pleased him.

Braden watched her, then rechecked her cinch. "Come on. Pete'll have some food for us. Pick up some saddlebags and stuff 'em full. Don't pay any attention to his disposition."

She followed Braden into the cabin. Sure enough, Pete was already filling the bags with jerky and biscuits. He tossed her old blanket at her. "Here. Don't leave this. Boys is liable to get lice from it."

Since Shelby had no strings on her saddle, Braden tied it on behind his. Pete followed them outside and stood scowling at the darkening sky. "You best move right along. Looks like we're in for more snow. Good thing there's stations close along the way. If things get too bad, you'll always have a place to hole up 'til it passes."

Shelby smiled as she mounted. He wasn't so terrible after all. Just another hard-bitten man afraid to reveal his more gentle side.

## CHAPTER 6

THEY RODE FOR A DISTANCE INTO THE DESERT, and when the wind died down enough so it didn't drive the words back into her mouth, Shelby ventured a question. "Did you think them men that stayed on at Pete's looked like stock tenders?"

"No. I've been thinking about them. Neece said he was short-handed and didn't think he'd get any better offers for help. But I know Major Egan won't be pleased that he hired two such obvious incompetents."

"I think they came out here with the idea they'd get hired. Like they knew there would be jobs waitin' for 'em," Shelby said.

"Seemed that way, all right. Elwood P. Hawker bothers me, too. Why would a drummer selling dress shoes come out into this wilderness? Surely he knew that if the stagecoach didn't run through this area, there couldn't be much civilization and little chance for a sale. I'm convinced there is some sort of plot to keep the Pony from running, but I keep missing parts to the puzzle. Can't seem to come up with proof. Just keep getting hunches."

"Don't suppose what happened to my pa had anything to do with any of this, do you?"

"Since this is the first time we've been alone without danger of someone overhearing, suppose you tell me your story," Braden invited. "Might be a piece to add to what I already suspicion."

Shelby started from the time her aunt died until the freight wagon stopped for her. She told the story in its entirety, taking pains to conceal her true identity. This seemed hardly the time or place to inform Braden that she was not a boy at all, but a girl, especially since they would be traveling together for at least two or three more days. She was, however, growing more and more uncomfortable with the deception and wanted to be free of it as soon as possible. Perhaps when they reached Carson City and before he tried to find her a job, she could tell him.

The wind picked up again and it began to snow. They raced for the station at Simpson's Park. Shelby couldn't remember when she'd ever been colder. The old coat with its missing button offered no resistance against the gale force buffeting them, and she shivered. Her face turned numb and she was fast losing the feeling in her feet and hands.

Suddenly Braden reined in his horse, and Shelby, riding in a stupor, galloped on past. He rode up beside her, grabbed her reins, and pulled her little mare to a halt, then tied her reins to his saddle horn. "Get on behind me," he commanded.

Shelby was too tired to argue and too cold to move. She kicked her feet free of the stirrups, and Braden scooped her out of her saddle and onto the skirt of his.

"Pull your hands up into your sleeves and put your arms around me, tight."

She did as he ordered and felt his elbows clamp against his sides and over her arms. His mustang objected to the added weight and did some fancy stepping to show his displeasure. Braden, however, soon had the horse straightened out into a brisk canter.

Pulling a scarf up over his face and ears so that all that showed were his eyes, Braden said, "When we stop tonight, sew a button on that coat and get a scarf and some gloves."

*Sure, I'll just run over to the store and buy those little luxuries. I imagine the selection is limitless,* she thought sarcastically.

Protected from the cold blast of the wind by Braden's body, Shelby soon could feel his warmth seeping through to her. She still couldn't feel anything from her knees down, but her hands began prickling painfully as they thawed. In a little while the prickling stopped, and warm and relaxed, she grew drowsy.

"Shelby!" Braden shouted.

Startled, she jerked awake. "What?" she yelled back.

"Don't go to sleep!" he barked. "It's a long way to the ground."

What was he talking about? His mount was a short-legged mustang. She opened her eyes and peered about. They were winding their way down a canyon wall, and the drop to the floor below was several hundred feet. She tightened her grip, turned her head away, and buried her face in his back. *Please, Lord, keep this little horse on the trail. I'm not ready to die just yet.*

"But don't hang on too tight," he gasped. "I need a little breathing room."

Reluctantly she loosened her arms slightly and felt his ribs move against them. She must have grown stronger in these past few weeks of manual labor and took some small comfort in the fact.

It was nearing dark when they arrived at Simpson's Park. "We're going to stay here tonight. It's only a swing station where the riders change horses, so he won't have as much room as a home station. We can bunk down by the fire, though. Better that than being out in this wind." Braden rode up to the cabin, leaned over, and beat on the door. "Alcott! Jim Alcott!"

The door flew open and they found themselves looking down the barrel of a rifle.

"Put that thing down! It's me, Braden Russell."

"Well, why didn't you say so? It's hard to tell who a man is when he's ridin' a strange horse, got a kid tacked on behind, and all you can see is his squinty little eyes. Shoulda knowed it was you. Only man in these parts dumb enough to be out in weather like this," Alcott snorted. "Get off and come in. I'll have the stock tender take care of your horses. He needs the practice."

Shelby watched Alcott reach out and lean the gun against the inside wall then turn to help her dismount. She couldn't move so he unlocked her fingers and broke the grip of her rigid arms. She fell into Alcott's waiting hands, but when her feet touched the ground, she could feel nothing. Her knees buckled. Braden slid off and caught her before she could hit the dirt.

"Kid got frostbit?" Alcott asked.

"I'm not sure. He's been awfully cold. Not enough warm clothes. We'll check him over as soon as we get in by the fire," Braden said and pushed through the open door.

Soon Shelby was stretched out on a cot by the fire. The rest of the evening was a blur. She remembered being wrapped in warm blankets and Braden forcing her to stay awake while he fed her hot barley and meat soup. She couldn't keep her eyes open after she finished eating, and the talk around the supper table was still going strong when she fell fast asleep.

The next morning Alcott rustled up some clothes for her. Though they were no cleaner than those she had on, they were considerably warmer. The things she had been wearing for three weeks were too ragged to stand washing, so she burned them.

Though the weather had not improved since yesterday, Braden was determined to push on. They made good time and stayed the next night at the Cold Springs Station, but a blinding blizzard forced them to stop early on the third day at Jim McNaughton's Station at Sand Springs.

"If this storm is hittin' the Sierras as hard as it is here, the boy carryin' the mail is going to have a trip to remember," Jim observed as he cut out the biscuits for supper and placed them on a cookie sheet.

"I don't think there's any doubt about it," Braden said, making no effort to hide his concern. "A miserable way to start the venture, isn't it?"

Jim slapped steaks into the hot greased skillet and their sizzle and aroma filled the cabin. "Who's carryin' the mail across the mountains?" he asked.

"Warren Upson."

"Good choice," Jim agreed. "Knows those mountains like the back of his hand and can ride like an Indian."

While the men visited, Shelby huddled near the fire, trying to rub the feeling back into her toes and fingers. Even with the warmer clothes, she had still felt like an ice sculpture at the end of the day's ride.

The trip the next day wasn't so long. In the early afternoon, they rode along the top of a narrow, steep-walled canyon where the Carson River flowed, and Braden pointed out Williams' Station.

"Are we going to spend the night here?" Shelby asked.

"Not if we don't have to." Braden's reply was curt.

Shelby wondered if she'd said something to irritate him, but in the past he'd always let her know promptly and plainly when he was displeased with her. She decided his present dour mood had something to do with either the storm or the weather.

They dropped down to the river bottom and then climbed the high knoll overlooking the stream. A column of smoke from the cabin chimney drifted lazily in the crisp, quiet air.

"What's this wagon road we're riding along?" she asked.

"California Trail," he answered without elaborating.

It was obvious Braden didn't wish to talk, so Shelby clamped her lips closed and kept them that way. There were a couple of canvas-covered wagons in the yard and several horses tied to the hitching rail. The corral held a number of ponies, some with the X.P. brand of the Pony Express.

Braden reined to a stop and Shelby pulled alongside. They tied their horses to the rail, and she followed Braden into the combination grog shop and trading station. Dimly lit, it was a few minutes before Shelby could make out the occupants—men standing at the bar and tired women and children hunched over a table.

As they entered, there seemed to be an argument in progress, and all attention was focused on a young Paiute warrior at the end of the bar. In response to someone's question, he shook his head vigorously and set a gun, five cans of powder, and five boxes of caps back on the counter.

"No lead, no pony," he stated flatly.

Braden strode into the midst of the discussion. "What's going on here, Williams?"

A man with a permanently tanned face and lines deeply etched around shifting eyes turned to Braden. "This Injun said he'd trade his pony for what you see before you. Now he wants five bars of lead to clinch the deal." Williams spat out the words.

Braden turned out to the Paiute and spoke in Shoshonee, the Indian's native language. They conversed briefly, then Braden faced Williams. "He says the lead was in the original deal and you didn't give it to him."

Williams's face twisted into ugly knots, and his eyes glittered hard as steel. "He lies! You gonna believe a thievin' Injun?"

In contrast Braden appeared stoic. There was no change of expression in the rugged features. "Where's his pony now?" he asked, his voice low and flat.

The other two Williams brothers came to stand shoulder to shoulder behind the bar. Shelby couldn't remember ever having seen three more threatening-looking men.

"The Injun said we could have it, so we took it to the barn," one of them said.

Slowly folding back his coat to expose his holster and flipping off the guard strap, Braden spoke each word in a measured staccato. "Go . . . get . . . it."

The room grew deathly quiet as the brothers moved as a phalanx from behind the bar and came to stand in front of Braden. "You're fast, Russell. But not fast enough to take three of us," the first man said, his lip curled in a sneer.

The wagon people, anticipating serious trouble, vanished out the door, and Shelby could hear the wagons clattering away. The miners and traders tensed with anticipation and moved out of the line of fire. Shelby didn't know what to do and stood frozen in her tracks in the middle of the room. *Dear God, don't let anything happen to Braden. Don't let anything happen to anyone. Please!*

Braden said something to the young brave and he left, reluctantly. Still staring at the three men, Braden spoke in a low voice, terrifying in its intensity. "Shelby, get out of here."

She obeyed. Once outside, she prayed fervently and watched the Indian stride toward the barn to retrieve his pony. As he came out leading a fine-looking animal, a snarling bundle of fur dashed out through the open station door and straight for the Indian. Grabbing the horse's mane, the young Paiute swung himself up, but not before the dog had sunk its teeth into his leg. He let out a startled yelp of pain, kicked his pony into a gallop, and dashed away into the desert.

Shelby stood in the wagon yard, shaken by what she had just witnessed. No wonder Braden didn't want to talk about Williams' Station. These men obviously made a habit of mistreating the Indians and probably any other unfortunates who came under their roof. Cruel laughter trailed through the still open door.

Braden stalked out. "Come on, Shelby, let's ride," he said as he stormed past her, untied his horse, and sprang into the saddle.

One of the Williams boys came out and called the dog back inside the trading post.

"That's right, leave, you Injun-lovin' squaw man!" he taunted.

The controlled impassiveness left Braden's face, and fury tightened its chiseled planes until his cheekbones stood out stark in the shadows cast by his wide-brimmed hat. His eyes held a dangerous gleam as he hauled his horse around to face the man.

"One day, Williams, you and your bloodsucking brothers are going to get yours. I hope I'm around when it comes." Braden's voice etched the words in the still, cold air.

A quick shudder ran through Shelby. She was glad when Braden booted his horse into a gallop and they could escape this evil place.

## CHAPTER 7

BRADEN TOOK THE TRAIL AT A FAST CLIP, hurrying Shelby along. This must be what it was like to carry the mail, she thought. She was beginning to get saddlesore, and a new set of muscles throbbed by the time Buckland's Station came into sight. She was nearing the end of her endurance.

"Why are we ridin' so fast?" she asked, suppressing the pain and weariness in her voice.

Apparently having recovered from his anger at the Williamses, Braden spoke in a conversational tone. "I want to be at Buckland's tonight when the first Pony rider comes in with the mail for the East. I expect he'll have a tale to tell."

Incredulous, she asked, "You mean one rider is goin' all the way to St. Joe?"

Much to her relief, Braden slowed his horse to a walk. "You obviously haven't been listening to the talk going on around you."

It was true. She hadn't been listening. Her own problems were far more pressing to her than the Indian troubles and silver strikes prevalent in Utah Territory gossip. None of it seemed to have any bearing on what had happened at Papa's mine, and the farther west they traveled, the less inclined Shelby felt to tune in to the conversation.

"I guess I don't understand what I hear," she said lamely.

"On April third, a rider started from St. Joe, Missouri, heading west," Braden proceeded to explain. "Another started from San Francisco the same day, going east. At the home stations, like Buckland's, the rider gives the mochila to another rider who takes it on to the next home station. When the two riders meet, one takes the mail going west, turns around and heads back the way he came. The other does the same. Each rider covers the same section of trail each time. That way they can become more familiar with the route and can make better time."

"So, sometimes a rider is carrying mail from the east and sometimes from the west?" Shelby asked, so intrigued that she lapsed into correct speech.

But apparently her oversight went unnoticed. "That's right," Braden continued. "We have eighty riders. Mail leaves once a week and takes about ten days to deliver. That's an incredibly fast speed. First time it's ever been done. Used to take a month or longer by stagecoach to get important mail across the continent."

Shelby rode along, trying to imagine all that had gone into organizing such an undertaking. "Has this mail thing been planned for a long time?"

"Since the last part of January."

"You mean all these stations, riders, horses, and supplies got put together in little more than two months?" Shelby could hardly believe it.

Braden shook his head. "Some of the stations were already here to serve freight wagons and emigrant trains, but most of them had to be built."

"Besides riding shotgun for Will's freight wagon, how are you involved?" Shelby realized she had broken a rule of western etiquette by prying into Braden's private life, but it was too late to call back the question.

He didn't look at her, and he didn't answer for a while, either. At last he said, "I run supply wagons from Carson

City out to the eastern desert stations. Raise mustangs on my ranch on the California side of the Sierras. Sold a sizable herd awhile back that was later sold to the Pony."

"You mean you could be riding your own horse?"

"Could be."

The brevity of his answer and the flat impersonal tone of his voice told Shelby that he was through answering questions of a private nature. The little she had learned about him had come in disconnected bits and pieces, and she kept track, trying to piece together his background. Now, however, was definitely time to take another line of questioning.

"Who's the brains and money behind the Pony?"

"Ever hear of the big freight outfit, Russell, Majors and Wadell?" The question was posed casually.

"Of course. They headquarter in my hometown, St. Joe."

"Right. Look up ahead." He pointed. "There's Buckland's."

Shelby craned her neck to catch sight of a rude log cabin standing in a beautiful grove of cottonwood trees where the river opened out into a meadow.

"Old Sam's a shrewd cuss. Got an excellent well with water that doesn't taste like alkali. This winter he built a toll bridge to bring the folks over from the California Trail. You can see it running along on the other side." Braden indicated a rough lumber bridge, yet unweathered, spanning the Carson River. "Sells them supplies, replacements for their trail-worn animals, and a tolerable quality and quantity of gut-warming whiskey over his bar. And he treats everyone fair, unlike some others I know."

They rode into the wagon yard and dismounted. Braden handed her the reins of his mustang. "You unsaddle the horses while I find out if there's room for us here tonight."

"That doesn't seem real smart." The comment slipped out before she thought better of it.

He stopped in his tracks and whirled around. "What did you say?" he thundered.

*Shelby, you idiot! He thinks you're fifteen. A fifteen-year-old who wants to keep his head attached to his shoulders wouldn't speak to an adult like that.*

She hung her head. "I'm sorry, sir," she said, trying to sound as contrite as she knew how.

"That's better. Anything I can't abide, it's a mouthy kid." But Braden gave her a long, speculative look before approaching the spot where she stood without moving, still clutching the reins of both horses. "Just what did you mean by that crack?"

Her eyes downcast, Shelby dug a hole with the toe of one boot and said in a small voice, "Just thought maybe you ought to find out if there's room for us *before* I unsaddle the horses."

He gave her a searching look, then threw back his head and laughed. "I hate to admit it, but you're right," he said, flipping off her hat and tousling her cropped hair. "Wait for me here, and I'll be back soon."

Shelby, anchored to the spot, watched in frustration as the wind rolled her hat along the frozen ground. "Braden, would you mind gettin' my hat 'fore it gets too far gone?" she called, resuming her boyish brogue.

Suddenly narrowing his eyes beneath scowling brows, he said, "Name's Mr. Russell to you."

Giving her a departing glare, he dashed in pursuit of the errant hat. Having retrieved it, he slapped it against his leg as he walked, dislodging the accumulated dirt and leaves. "Here," he said, and shoved the hat into her hands. "And in the future, remember all the training your good parents put in on you."

Before she could say anything, he stalked into the station and slammed the door.

"Shelby," she chided herself under her breath, "you're going to be afoot out in the cold if you don't keep your mouth under control. It hasn't been that long since you were fifteen. Surely you can remember how it was."

But Braden apparently planned to give her plenty of time to repent. It seemed hours before he returned. She was freezing by the time he threw open the door and came outside.

"You can unsaddle the horses now," he called to her. "The Pony rider is due in any time, but Sam says there'll be room for us."

Gratefully, Shelby nodded and hustled the horses into the corral. Her fingers, cold and stiff, responded awkwardly. Her horse stood easy, and the light Pony saddle which weighed only a third as much as a normal western saddle slid off with no problem. She deposited it over the corral fence and tackled Braden's mustang. But he was another matter. Even after all the miles they had traveled, the ornery little creature seemed as wild as when they had left Roberts' Creek Station.

"Hold still, you miserable excuse for a horse," she shouted at the mustang as he danced away from her. Crowding him against the corral fence, she was finally able to get the cinch unfastened and slide the saddle off. She hadn't lifted Braden's saddle before and when it came free, together with all the gear tied to it, and fell into her arms, she staggered beneath its weight.

"Oh, great gobs of little green grasshoppers!" she shouted.

At a laugh behind her, she whirled to see Braden, leaning his outstretched arms on the top rail of the corral and relaxing his booted foot on the bottom log of the fence.

"I'd have expected some stronger language under the circumstances," he said, smiling the first real smile she had seen from him.

"I don't swear, if that's what you mean," she retorted and at the moment didn't care if he did think she was a smart-mouthed brat.

He crawled between the logs and came to her rescue. "I don't relish my saddle being dropped in the manure," he said and grabbed it one-handed by the horn.

"If you're so worried about your precious saddle, then don't ask me to take it off your old horse. Especially when the saddle weighs half as much as I do," she snapped and grabbed her saddle off the fence. Without looking at him, she stormed around the corner of the cabin and unlatched the slab door. Retreating from the wind, she slammed the door behind her.

With all the people and a fire roaring, the interior of the cabin was hot and stuffy. Combined with the smell of unwashed bodies, sweaty clothes, stale tobacco smoke, sour whiskey, and freshly ground coffee, the blast of air that assailed her when she entered nearly knocked her down. Maybe the out of doors wasn't so bad, after all. At least there she could breathe.

Unnoticed in the excitement of the imminent arrival of the first eastbound Pony Express rider, Shelby found an unoccupied corner and dropped her saddle. Sitting down beside it, she sized up the place. Behind the bar must be the owner, Sam Buckland, a rawboned man with deep-set eyes. It was his eyes that held Shelby. They seemed to glow with a hidden madness. She would go out of her way to avoid him, she decided grimly.

"All right, boys! Step lively and get that pony saddled!" Buckland shouted over the din.

*Anything to escape this fetid air,* Shelby thought, leaping to her feet and joining the rush out the door. Once outside, they found Braden leaning up against the lee side of the building, holding the reins of the ready mustang prancing nervously in front of him.

A wiry young man bristling with a Spencer rifle and two Colt .44's, one holstered on each hip, and a bowie knife stuck in his belt, pushed his way through the crowd and stepped up next to Braden. They talked earnestly, but Shelby was too far away to hear what was being said. Braden began pointing, and she guessed he was telling of the trail they had just ridden.

At the cry, "Here he comes!", every head turned to watch the lone rider racing across the desert.

Sam Buckland came running out of the station. "Stand back!" he yelled. "Give him room! Don't crowd until we get Bartoles on his way east."

Shelby found herself shoved back against the cabin wall, unable to see anything. Using her size to advantage, she elbowed her way through and up to the front where there was a clear view. She watched the rider standing half out of his saddle, holding the reddish leather mochila with the rectangular boxes sewn into each corner. She recognized it immediately, for it was like the one she had ridden on. He had already removed it from the wooden saddle frame and had it ready to pass to the next rider.

"Throw it, Boston!" Braden shouted.

The light mochila came sailing through the air. Bartoles caught it and helped Braden hook it over the saddle horn and cantle of his saddle. Sam nervously fumbled the key into the lock of the local mail pouch. Removing the waybill, Sam penciled in Boston's arrival time, shoved the waybill back into the pouch, and quickly relocked the small padlock.

Boston brought his lathered pony to a halt, but before he stepped out of the saddle, Bartoles was already galloping off on his way east to Williams' Station. There he would get a fresh horse and continue his race out into the desert.

"That change took less than a half a minute!" cried someone in the crowd.

Loud cheers went up from the waiting group and they gathered around Boston to usher him inside.

"What news do you bring?" Shelby heard Braden ask as she kept close on his heels.

She needed to learn all she could, for Braden had suggested that she might be able to get a job with the Pony because of her slight build, that is, if she could ride well enough. Thanks to her papa's tutoring, she knew she could pass that requirement.

Just before she entered the warm room, she turned for one more uncontaminated breath. There stood the overheated horse, tied to the hitching rail, taking the full brunt of the sharp wind. She flinched. The poor thing! Braden had told her the Pony owners spared no expense in buying the finest horseflesh available. Well, this was no way to protect their investment, she thought.

Shelby wheeled around and hurried up to the animal that was still panting from exertion. She untied the reins, climbed into the saddle, and began walking the horse around the wagon yard to cool him down. When he had cooled sufficiently, she allowed him to drink from a large rainbarrel, watching to be sure he did not consume too much. Finally she led him into the corral and removed the saddle. The mustang wouldn't stand for any more fuss, though, and when she tried to brush him, he bucked and whinnied, heading out into the throng of milling animals.

There was nothing else to be done for him, but she did wish it would warm up a bit. She dreaded going back into that unventilated saloon. As she passed the door, Braden came out.

"What have you been up to?" he asked.

"Somebody had to take care of the horse. I thought you said all the stations had stock tenders. This one either don't have none, or he don't know his job."

"He's around, but I have a feeling he was too excited to remember why he'd been hired. Everyone but you is inside listening to Boston tell about Warren Upson's hair-raising crossing of the Sierras."

"If Boston left as soon as the other rider got there, how does he know so much?" she asked, not much impressed. "I'd rather hear the story from Warren Upson. Secondhand ain't the same."

Braden regarded her carefully. "You're the strangest kid. You stay outside to worry over the horse and then don't even want to hear what happened."

"I am not strange," she objected. "You keep tellin' me how much the owners paid for these here horses, and then everybody goes off and leaves a hot horse standin' in this freezin' wind. *That's* strange, if you ask me!" She was getting thoroughly miffed at his constant references to her behavior this evening. "If he thinks acting like a boy is easy, he ought to try it," she said in a low voice and stomped off toward the river. As she neared the bridge, she realized what she had said, and it sounded so ridiculous she stopped to chuckle.

"You got a quarter?" Braden shouted after her.

"You know I don't!" She whirled around to face him.

"Then I wouldn't advise walking across that bridge," he said as he ambled toward her.

"You mean it costs a quarter to go to the other side?" Her eyes widened in disbelief.

"Sure does." He put an arm around her shoulders and firmly pushed her toward the cabin. "Now stop being so stubborn and come inside out of this wind."

She tried ducking from under his grasp, but he held her tight. She struggled against him. "I don't want to go back in that stinkin' place. It makes me sick to my stomach."

He glared down at her. "And where do you propose to stay?"

"I don't know, but ain't there any place to sleep but in a bar?" Shelby was close to tears and hoped Braden would think it was the wind in her eyes. "How's Boston goin' to get any rest?"

"Don't worry. Sam'll shut everything down at nine. Those who want, can spend the night here. The rest will go back across the river to their own camps or wagons. Supper's about ready. You've earned your keep by taking care of that horse. Come on in. You'll feel better with some hot beans in your belly."

Grudgingly, Shelby allowed him to guide her into the cabin. "How long are we goin' to stay here?" she asked when they were settled at a table.

"Until tomorrow. I need to get to Carson City. There we'll have accommodations that should please you. You can even take a bath." He paused and looked her over. "In fact, I insist you take one. We'll see if we can find you a job there. Maybe get an advance on your first wages and buy you some new clothes."

Shelby wasn't paying much attention to what Braden said after the word *bath*. She was already lost in the feel of her body submerged in hot soapy water.

## CHAPTER 8

SHELBY AND BRADEN ENTERED CARSON CITY from the northeast and rode down the main street. It seemed years since Shelby had seen so much civilization, and as they rode past the fine hotels, boarding houses, saloons, and stores, she gaped like a kid in town for the first time.

She grew nervous as Braden kept riding, ignoring all the places to stop. At last she could keep quiet no longer. "Ain't you aimin' to find a place to stay the night?"

He looked at her from under a hat pulled far forward. "I am, but not here. They're probably full anyway." He pushed his pony a bit ahead of hers, a sign that he was through talking and she'd better hush and follow.

The streets were muddy from the last storm, but the frost in the ground kept them from wallowing in thick ooze. She imagined that when spring brought the first thaw, these streets would be nearly impassable. Nevertheless, this city, a new settlement on the way to the Comstock Lode, had been carefully laid out, unlike many of the towns they had visited. The wide streets intersected at regular intervals, and Shelby saw that she and Braden were fast approaching a large, empty plaza. For the first time she could see no logic in the plan.

"Mr. Russell!" she called.

He reined back and let her catch up.

"Why ain't anything built on that block of land right in the middle of town?"

"Abe Curry, who planned Carson City, reserved that spot for the state capitol."

"State capitol? Ain't this still part of the Utah Territory?"

"For now, but there's a big move afoot to have it declared the Nevada Territory. Now that we have fast mail to the East, it could happen soon."

Shelby was still chewing on this bit of information when Braden pulled up in front of a large adobe building, two stories high. *Ormsby House* was printed in large black letters along the side. He swung out of the saddle and wrapped the reins around the hitching rail. Shelby sat gaping at the splendid place, which would be considered fine even in St. Joe. Out here its grandeur was totally unexpected.

"You coming in or do you want to sit admiring the outside awhile longer?" he asked as he untied his saddle roll.

Without taking her eyes from the building for fear it might disappear, Shelby dismounted. She reached to take her blanket from him.

"Leave it," Braden ordered. "It needs to be burned along with your clothes."

"I realize it ain't much, but it's all I got. After you burn everything, what am I gonna do?" she wailed.

"You see that store?"

She looked at the store attached to the Ormsby House. "They take charity cases?"

"Not without good references," he said, and stepped up onto the wooden veranda running in front of the hotel.

Shelby stood beside her horse, watching his retreating figure. He placed his hand on the doorknob and looked around. His eyebrows drew together in a frown. "Your feet not working today, boy?"

"You want me to go in that beautiful hotel like . . . like this?" she said, holding her hands palms outward in a gesture of helplessness.

"Not really, but at the moment there don't seem a great many choices."

Shelby smashed her hat as far over her face as she could and trudged through the mud to the porch. She looked down, chagrined at the footprints that followed her to the front door.

Braden also noticed the trail. "Wipe off your feet," he scolded.

Shelby looked all around. "Where?"

"There." He pointed to a metal scraper mounted near the door.

She was so flustered she had missed it. Under his glowering scrutiny, she tried to remove the mud, but it stuck like glue. She looked up to meet his scowl and seeing him so upset with her, her lower lip began to tremble. "It won't come off."

"If you watched where you walked, you wouldn't collect the whole street on your boots. Take them off. You can't walk on Elizabeth's floor with those filthy things."

Shelby struggled to remove the offending boots. "Who's Elizabeth?" She ventured a timid question.

"Elizabeth Ormsby, wife of the Major William Ormsby who built this place."

"Oh," Shelby sighed with relief and then wondered at her sudden concern. *You can fool Braden, Shelby, but you can't lie to yourself.* She had been afraid Elizabeth might be a beautiful single woman waiting for Braden's return.

The first boot hit the porch with a solid thud, and Shelby inspected the toes showing through the end of her sock.

"Take the sock off too."

"Go in barefooted?"

He nodded and watched her remove the other boot and sock. She tucked the socks inside the boots and started to carry them inside.

"Set them by the wall. I'll send someone for them."

She did as Braden bade, rolled up her pants legs a couple of turns, and followed him into the immaculately clean and tastefully appointed lobby. A dainty bell rang, announcing their entrance, and a gracious woman in a flowered calico dress swept through an arched doorway to greet them.

"Braden!" A wide smile lit her face, and she clasped his hand in greeting. "William and I had about given you up as lost." She slipped her hand over his arm, and together they walked slowly toward the desk. Long dark ringlets, tied back with a bright yellow ribbon, covered her head that barely came to Braden's shoulder. The curls flipped in a fetching manner as she continued her animated dialogue. "William is out on business, but I expect him back shortly. He'll be delighted to see you. He has much to talk over with you."

Braden gave Elizabeth his full attention. "It's good to be back. I've had a long trip, but I did locate the stagecoach driver who witnessed my family's massacre. Unfortunately, he wasn't much help." His somber mood lightened. "However, we were at Buckland's in time to see the Pony come through."

"Oh, my goodness, but that must have been an exciting moment!" Her voice bubbled with vitality.

It was obvious that here was a woman who had everything she wanted and the good sense to appreciate it. Shelby looked enviously at the two friends still clasping hands.

"We need a bath and a room, preferably one with two beds," Braden informed Elizabeth.

At the mention of *we,* she noticed Shelby standing far back in the lobby. Giving Shelby a long searching look, Elizabeth said, "Bath, indeed! And some clean clothes, I'd say."

Braden followed Elizabeth's gaze. "I shall leave the choice of clothes up to you, but don't make them fancy. Shelby is going to apply for work with the Pony as a stock tender. By the way, the boy's boots are outside."

"Thank you for that."

Shelby felt as if Elizabeth wished Braden had also left *her* on the doorstep.

"I understand Bolivar Roberts still needs some

hands," the woman said, turning her full attention again to Braden. "There are plenty of applicants for riders, but as usual, nobody wants to do the dirty work."

Braden turned to Shelby. "Hear that, kid? You'll have a job by dinner tomorrow."

Shelby nodded and tried to look pleased at the news. However, she was growing very tired of being a boy, particularly after seeing the lovely Mrs. Ormsby and remembering how nice cambric underthings felt next to the skin.

Elizabeth went behind the desk and produced the hotel register. She studied it, a slight frown marring her creamy white forehead. "We're awfully full right now, Braden. The best I can give you is a small room with a double bed. The two of you will have to share for a couple of nights."

Shelby heard nothing more. Share a bed with Braden?! *But I can't do that!* she thought, horrified. *There has to be a way out of this! It's early yet. Maybe someone will check out or fail to show up*, Shelby assured herself. *Or maybe I should simply tell Elizabeth the truth. She'd understand.* Shelby eyed her speculatively. On second thought, what woman would believe such a tale? Especially when she learned of the nights Shelby and Braden had slept around a campfire with only coyotes for chaperones.

*What will Braden do when he learns I'm a girl? What kind of a job will I get then? You'd better keep things just the way they are until you have a better option, my girl,* she told herself.

"Shelby!"

Braden's voice roused her from her reverie. "Huh?" she asked stupidly, wondering what had been said to her.

"Elizabeth wants to know what size boot you take?"

Shelby panicked. She knew what size she required in women's shoes, but she had no idea how boy's sizes ran.

"Uh," she hesitated, holding up a grimy foot for inspection, "I grew some, so I don't rightly know, ma'am." *Thank you, Lord, for those words.*

Elizabeth looked with distaste at Shelby's dirty foot.

"Well, take your bath, and when you're clean, we'll go over to the store for a fitting." Dismissing Shelby, she turned to Braden. "I'll have water heated and sent right down. Want a cup of coffee in the kitchen while you wait? We can visit. I'm anxious to hear about your adventures."

Braden tossed the key and his bedroll to Shelby. "Here, kid. Take this to the room, but don't touch anything. You're going to need a complete scrubdown before you're fit for civilization."

He disappeared through the arched doorway, leaving Shelby standing alone in the lobby. She had grown thoroughly tired of hearing how dirty she was. The condition certainly wasn't by choice.

And where was the room? She peered through an open doorway, but from the number of newspapers lying about, and chairs arranged for the best light, she quickly concluded this was the reading room. She felt curious eyes on her and turned in that direction. There, behind the counter of the aromatic corner tobacco shop, stood a man. His eyes looked on her in a friendly fashion, and this restored a bit of her self-confidence.

"The door you want is to the right of the counter. Your room's the last one on the first floor in the corner," he said in a quiet voice.

"Thanks, mister," she said, grateful for his help.

"Name's Chandler. Stop by anytime."

Acknowledging his offer with a nod of her head, Shelby pushed through a wide door and trudged down a long hall. When she found the room, she inserted the key in the lock. It turned easily, but before opening the door, Shelby inspected her hand. It was grayish black from ground-in dirt and splotched with dried blood from untended cracks due to the cold. The nails were ragged and broken. Disgusting! Were boys always so dirty? She recalled that her cousins were, unless forced to be otherwise.

Wiping the offending hand down the side of her pants, Shelby opened the door. Once inside, she understood Braden's concern. The room was spotless and decorated with lovely carpets, quilts, and dainty crocheted doilies, the kind of place Shelby longed to have for her own. Her fingers fairly itched to touch the crystal prisms hanging from the lamps and relish the sleekness of the satin pillows adorning the bed. Over the rosewood chest was a fine gilt mirror, but Shelby avoided it. Her hair was stringy with dirt and grease, and her face, impregnated with alkali dust. Looking in the mirror would serve only to verify her sad deterioration.

She didn't dare sit or lean, and so she stood in the middle of the floor. After a while, she heard footsteps coming down the hall and pausing outside the room. A light tap on the door announced that someone was about to enter. She watched the knob turn and the door swung open, admitting a slender young man carrying a copper tub. He spread oilcloth on the floor and set the tub in the middle, then walked up to her, eyeing her thoroughly as he did so.

"One change of water ain't gonna be enough for you," he said. "You stink!"

Shelby smarted under his words. "Nobody invited you. If you don't like the smell, you can leave!"

"I'm plannin' to. Here's your towels." He tossed several large white ones on the bed and pranced out, leaving the door ajar.

Shelby stormed over and booted it shut with her foot. Then, standing with arms folded over her chest, she glared at the barrier. If she could stay angry enough, maybe she wouldn't cry.

The same young man returned with the hot water, followed by Braden and Elizabeth. Braden's face showed more animation than at any time since Shelby had met him, though she had to admit it would be difficult to remain sullen in the presence of such buoyant good spirits as Elizabeth displayed. But they all ignored Shelby as they prepared the bath.

"How does the temperature seem to you?" Elizabeth asked Braden.

He stuck in a cautious finger. "A bit on the warm side, but leave a pitcher of cold water and I can cool it if I have to." He dropped his heavy coat on the floor and began unbuttoning his shirt.

As she was leaving, Elizabeth turned her attention briefly to Shelby. "When he's finished, use his water. That'll take off the first layers. Then we'll send in fresh water."

"Thank you," Shelby said sincerely. It seemed to Shelby that Elizabeth looked on her more kindly than in the lobby. Braden had undoubtedly told her how he had come to have a ragamuffin tagging along.

Elizabeth closed the door, and Shelby could hear her footsteps retreating down the hall. Panic mounted as she realized she was in the room alone with a man who was stripping in preparation for a bath. In desperation, she sought the place farthest from the tub, a lone window on the opposite side of the room. Automatically she reached to pull back the white lace curtains.

"Don't touch those!" Braden thundered.

Still facing the window, she jumped back and dropped her hands to her sides. She stood motionless as grunts and mutterings issued from Braden's corner of the room. At last, a boot hit the floor. More sounds of a struggle filled the room. "Give me a hand, will you?" he gasped.

She hurried to stand in front of a red-faced Braden, tugging unsuccessfully on the second boot. He thrust his foot forward, and bracing herself, Shelby gripped the toe and heel and reared back. She felt the boot give, but not in time to catch her balance and she catapulted backward, landing in a heap on the floor.

Alarm spread over Braden's face. "You all right, kid?"

Quickly she bounded to her feet. "Yeah," she said in a rough voice, trying to hide her embarrassment. "If you'd wear socks with heels in 'em, the boots would come off easier." How good it felt to give him a taste of his own medicine.

He hastened to take off the offending articles and tossed them in the corner. "I'll get some new ones at the store in the morning," he mumbled.

Shelby picked up the boots and placed them as a pair

under the window. Now she could hear the small clink of his belt buckle and the soft pop of buttons as Braden unfastened his pants. *How am I going to get out of here?* she thought. *I can't stay here while he bathes.* Her palms were growing sweaty. *This is awful. Just awful!* The buckle continued to clink slightly over the rustle of cloth as he pushed the trousers down his legs. The floor boards protested with tiny squeaks as he shifted his weight to step out of first one leg, and then the other. *Oh,* she wailed silently. *Dear Lord, what am I going to do?* The buckle clunked as the pants hit the floor.

There came a small plinking sound. *He's testing the water with his foot.* She bit her lip to keep it from trembling. Why hadn't she told him who she was? How long did she think she could keep up this masquerade without getting caught? But after this incident, how could she tell him?

She wanted to die. Maybe if she stood closer to the window, a stray bullet might somehow strike her down. Tears filled her eyes and blurred her vision. Slowly she sank cross-legged to the floor on the other side of the bed from Braden's tub and rested her chin on her hands. She clenched her eyes shut and felt the tears that refused to stop drip onto her hands and run down her arms. How she wished to be anywhere but here!

A contented "Ah!" told her the water temperature was to his liking and Braden was settled. He washed long and vigorously with such splashings and blowings she wasn't sure any water would be left in the tub.

"Kid, you still here?" he asked at last.

"I'm here."

"Come wash my back. Haven't had that luxury in a long time."

Shelby froze, praying she'd only imagined his request.

"Kid?"

"Y—yes?"

"Are you coming?"

"Su—sure." Shelby kept her eyes glued to the scene through the window—the side of another building.

"What's the matter with you?"

*Oh, dear Lord, please help me!* "Well, I, uh, wasn't sure you wanted my dirty hands in your bath water."

"Not particularly, but it'll be a start on getting them clean."

Shelby swallowed the knot in her throat, and keeping her eyes averted, eased around the bed in the direction of his voice. She saw the edge of the oilcloth and carefully ran her eyes along its bright yellow surface until she came to the bottom of the tub. She traced the edge of the tub until it made a wide curve near where she stood. Her heart gave a leap. His back was to her. *Thank the Lord!*

"Where's the washcloth?" she asked, trying to sound as casual as possible.

"Right here." He tossed a wet ball over his shoulder. "I like lots of soap."

She located the soap floating in a saucer. Kneeling, she remoistened the cloth and soaped it until it foamed luxuriously. He leaned forward, exposing the long length of his well-muscled back. Having seen only her thin, scrawny papa and her little cousins as children bathing at the pump, she was unprepared for the sight of wide sinewy shoulders that tapered along rippling muscles to a narrow waist. *Lord, forgive me!* she begged, blushing furiously, *but what was I supposed to do?*

"Where you want me to start?" she asked.

"Common sense says to start at the top and wash down. I don't know about you, kid." He shook his head and turned to regard her over his shoulder.

His inference irked her. "I don't usually scrub backs, Mr. Russell. But when I have, *sir,* I've taken note that people have certain druthers, like starting with the left shoulder, or the right shoulder, or the back of the neck. Now, Mr. Russell, *sir,* you got any druthers?" Her voice dripped with sarcasm.

He chuckled low in his throat. "Well put, Shelby Jackson. I had that coming. Actually, I've never really thought a lot about where a back washing should begin, but there's an itch on my left shoulder which seems to indicate that might be the place to start."

"Yes, sir." Shelby fortified herself with a deep breath and attacked with all the vigor at her command.

"Hey, take it easy. I'd like a little skin left when you're through."

She eased up some, but only after his back was a bright red from the scrubbing. She filled the cloth with water and rinsed off the soap.

"There. How does that feel?"

"Like I'd been rubbed down with a pumice stone. I can hardly wait to repay you." He caught the washcloth as she tossed it back to him.

"What do you mean—repay me?" she asked as she stood and quickly returned to her spot at the window.

"I haven't forgotten how devious young boys can be, and your penchant for dirt says I'd better supervise and assist with your scouring."

Shelby gasped and gripped the front of her shirt. "I don't need no help. I can scrub myself."

Water sloshed loudly as Braden stood up. "I'm sure you can, but I'm not sure you *will*, and I'll not have you appearing in public one more day looking like an unsupervised waif. You're an embarrassment to me. Makes me look like an unfit father."

"*Father!*" Shelby whirled on him, forgetting his unclothed condition. He was standing in a neatly wrapped towel, combing his hair at the mirror.

"Yes. Father. I've been giving your situation much thought, and Elizabeth agrees with me. You can't simply run loose. No way of knowing all the trouble you'd get in to." As he talked, he struggled to pull the comb through the tangle of curls and winced with pain at each tug. "You seem to come from good stock and could amount to something if given the right set of circumstances."

Shelby was struck dumb. She didn't want him for a father. She wanted to say, *Look, Braden, I'm a girl. Reasonably attractive, strong, healthy. I think you're wonderful, and I'd like to suggest the right set of circumstances*. But instead, she stared at him, knowing if he could read her mind, he'd throw her out on her ear, and she'd deserve it for having deceived him so long. *Please Lord, I don't know what to do. I'm scared to tell him the truth. I need your help desperately. Things are getting way out of hand.*

His hand paused in midair. "You don't like the idea?" he asked, half-turning to catch her reaction.

"What idea?" she stalled.

"Having me for a father. I realize I have no experience along those lines, except for having been a kid once myself." He didn't sound quite so confident.

"Oh, sir, it isn't that. You'd be a fine father. Really fine," she hastened to assure him. "But you're gone so much of the time. What would you do with me?"

"Put you with some good folks on the Pony route. Let you work for your keep. I'd be by real often since I'm keeping the route under constant watch."

She thought about it. "You're sayin' you'd keep an eye on me 'til I get growed enough to take care of myself?"

He returned to the work of combing his hair. "Something like that."

She couldn't stand the way he was abusing those lovely dark curls. She marched over and took the comb from his hand. "Sit down and let me comb your hair before you pull it all out."

He turned shocked eyes on her. "Just who do you think you're bossing around, young man?"

Shelby could have bitten out her tongue. "S—sorry, sir," she said, hanging her head.

He laughed and tousled her hair. The air between them was suddenly charged, and the laugh died on his lips. She wanted to throw her arms around him and hug him, smell the clean pungent soap smell lingering on his skin, have him put his arms around her and hold her tight. She kept her head down so he wouldn't read all those thoughts in her eyes.

*Oh Lord, help me. What am I to do?* She was going to have to tell him. It wasn't fair. But when she did, he would feel betrayed, and in his anger, he would wash his hands of her. She knew him well enough now to anticipate some of his reactions. She took a deep breath and gripped the comb in an attempt to gather her courage.

A sharp knock on the door shattered the silence. "Come in!" Braden bellowed.

The young man who had been serving them cracked open the door and stuck a worried face around the corner. "Anything wrong?" he asked in a timid voice.

"No!" Braden growled. "What do you want, Henry?"

Shelby watched Henry's Adam's apple nervously bob up and down, and then she looked at Braden. His face was a black thundercloud and his eyes shot fire. No wonder the poor kid was scared. Anyone with sense would be.

Henry licked his lips and thrust a heavily laden arm through the door. "I . . . I have your clothes, sir."

"Put them on the bed," Braden ordered. "Anything else?"

"Y—yes, sir. Major Ormsby asks that you join him in the reading room as soon as you're dressed." He laid a fine black suit and starched white shirt on the bed and set polished black leather dress boots on the floor. "Mrs. Ormsby sent this robe for your young man to put on when he's through bathing." Henry thrust the robe at Shelby. "He's to throw his old clothes out the window and report to her for a complete outfitting." Under Braden's dark scowl, Henry scurried to the door, eager to have his business concluded. "One more thing," he said to Shelby just before he slipped out. "Mrs. Ormsby says you better be scrubbed clean or she'll set you back in that tub and take over the job herself. And if you don't believe she would, you don't know her!"

Shelby nodded dumbly. Looking forlornly at the already well-used water, a small sigh escaped. Braden followed her gaze.

"Looks a bit thick, doesn't it?" In two quick strides, he had the door open. "Henry," he bellowed, "bring Shelby a fresh tub of water, now!"

Back at her window, Shelby had a great urge to cry. With Braden's every thoughtful act, her insides were twisting more and more. She blinked back tears, knowing if they spilled over, they'd leave telltale streaks in the dirt. Besides, big boys didn't cry.

In the background she could hear the sounds of Braden dressing. Then he began muttering.

"What's the matter?" she asked, turning around to see him bent double.

His words were a bit muffled as he peered under the bed. "I can't find my comb, and I sure can't go in public with my hair like this."

Shelby glanced down. She was still clutching the comb. "I have it," she said in a weak voice.

"That's right. You were going to show me how to manage unruly hair." Braden straightened up and raked impatient fingers through his mop as he sat on the only chair. "Well, have at it," he said, his voice unusually gruff.

She couldn't move for staring at him. She had always thought him reasonably good-looking even in trail clothes, but now . . . he looked so handsome in his ruffled shirt, black pants and tie, it took her breath away.

Nervously he ran his thumbs under his dark suspenders. "Something the matter?"

"Oh, no," she breathed. "You look wonderful. Really important—like a senator or a bank president or something." She stuck out the comb. "I'd better not get close to you. I might shed or molt or be contagious."

A slow grin eased over his face, creasing deep crevices into his cheeks. Even his normally expressionless eyes glowed slightly. "You're all right, Shelby Jackson." He took the comb and forced the curls into submission. One escaped onto his forehead but he left it. Shelby was glad he did. It gave Braden a certain jaunty air and suited him perfectly. He slipped into the carefully tailored cutaway jacket and adjusted the shoulders. Giving himself one final appraisal in the mirror, he moved to the door.

"Sorry I can't stay and scrub your back, but you'd better heed Henry's warning. Elizabeth's favorite places to check, I'm told, are behind the ears and the back of the neck."

Shelby grinned. "Thanks. I'll scrub especially hard there."

He opened the door and gave a little wave as he disappeared down the hall.

"Uh . . . thanks for the clean water," she called after him.

He turned and stood looking at her—the most attractive, genuinely good man she'd ever known. He nodded slowly, then continued on his way. She watched, her heart beating an erratic pattern, until he disappeared through the door at the end of the hall.

## CHAPTER 9

AT THE ORMSBY HOUSE, completed by the Major and Elizabeth in the fall of 1859 and elegantly decorated, dinner was always something special. At those infrequent moments, when Braden took time out from his pursuit of those who were trying to ruin him and the Pony, he dwelled on the pleasant evenings spent there. Tonight, as he and William entered, Elizabeth was already seating the guests, and the table was nearly full.

Braden cast about for Shelby. That kid was the biggest bundle of contradictions he'd ever run across. One minute, he was a mouthy brat, and Braden wanted to smack him. The next, he was humble, pathetic, defeated, and Braden could hardly fight down the irrational desire to hold and comfort him.

Braden was still having trouble dealing with the earlier scene in their bedroom. Every time he touched the kid, something extraordinary happened. Was this the way you felt about your children? He meant to ask William, but it had to be done casually so as not to arouse undue speculation.

Now, as he took his place at the table, he scanned the lodgers who were already seated. Where was that kid? *I'll tan his hide good if he's late for dinner. I knew I never should have left him to dress by himself.*

Braden was working himself up to a fine rage when his eyes fell on a little body with a bowed head of golden brown hair, trying to shrink into oblivion. Seated across and down the table from Braden, the unrecognizable Shelby was dressed in a new white shirt and black tie. Shiny hair was parted in the middle and pulled behind small delicate ears still glowing pink from a recent scrubbing.

After William pronounced the blessing, Braden, seated next to Elizabeth, asked in a low voice, "Is that Shelby?"

Looking very pleased with herself, Elizabeth nodded. "I had the Devil's own time getting him dressed, though. Held the clothes up to test the size, but refused to try on anything but the boots in my presence. Took everything back to your room and came to the table dressed as you see him."

"You think his behavior is normal?" Braden asked.

"Completely, unfortunately."

"I seem to remember being like that," Braden nodded in acknowledgment. "Grown up one minute and thinking like an adult. The next, doing something so dumb my father would nearly explode from the urge to thump on me and send me to my room."

"Now, do us all a favor and don't forget how it felt at this age. Being a father is far from easy," Elizabeth said and smiled in Shelby's direction.

Braden felt himself color and nervously looked again toward the miserable little creature. However, Shelby was sitting up straight and handling the passing of the food with some degree of finesse and so far hadn't disgraced either of them.

Even though Elizabeth had taken care to seat a beautiful woman next to him, Braden wasn't enjoying the meal as usual. He couldn't keep his eyes from Shelby, even though the kid was doing everything right—eating like a well-mannered adult and speaking when spoken to. There was a grace and ease about the way he managed his utensils which bespoke fine training. Yet on the trail he'd been thoroughly boorish in his table behavior. He determined to speak to Shelby. No longer would such appalling manners be tolerated anywhere.

At last Braden dismissed Shelby from his mind and fell into conversation with Lila, his dinner companion. He heard for the first time of the murder in late March of a miner in the nearby hills. An Indian attack, it appeared from all reports, yet all they had taken was a sack of flour. Nevertheless, nearly everyone was in favor of wreaking vengeance on the Paiute Indians encamped at Pyramid Lake.

"Has anyone considered that the miners have chopped down the piñon trees which supply the Indians with the nuts forming the main staple of their diet? And butchered the deer and elk, heedless of the needs of the tribe?" Braden heard himself asking.

"That doesn't give them the right to go about murdering people," William retorted.

"If my family was hungry and that was the only way I could get food, I'm not so sure I'd be above the act. Besides, all you have is the story from the miner's grief-stricken brother."

"I always knew you favored Chief Numaga and his tribe, but I think you're carrying things a bit too far," William cautioned.

"Perhaps, but I don't intend to take one man's word as gospel against a people suffering from cold and starving by the scores and unable to do anything about it. Have you been out to Pyramid Lake to see their living conditions?" Braden felt himself growing defensive.

"No, and I wouldn't advise anyone to go. I understand there's talk of calling all the tribes together for a big powwow." William's voice carried its warning over the silent room.

Elizabeth interrupted the discussion that was becoming more heated than appropriate at dinner. "Has anyone heard the tale of Warren Upson's trip with the Pony Express mail?"

"It's a story worth hearing more than once!" William's voice boomed enthusiastically. "How that boy did it, I'll never know. Took the mail from William Hamilton at Sportsman's Hall on the other side of the Sierras and ran into one of the worst blizzards of the year in the mountains. Bolivar Roberts had teams of oxen tromping down the snow to keep the trail open for the stagecoach, but it was blowing and drifting, so even that didn't work for long."

"I was at the office when Upson rode in," someone said. "Boy said he'd ridden blind in subzero cold, with drifts higher than his head. Couldn't even make out landmarks he'd known for years, it was such a blizzard. Spent over a day making a trip that usually takes a couple of hours. Said it was the hardest eighty-five miles he ever rode or ever hoped to."

The talk settled into a less controversial vein, and as they were waiting for dessert to be served, Braden felt a pair of eyes on him. He turned slightly and looked directly into great liquid pools of emerald green, shining from a healthy glowing face. Why were such magnificent eyes wasted on that little squirt of a boy? In a girl, fringed as they were with thick curling brown lashes, they would be positively devastating. Particularly if managed knowingly from behind a fan as Lila so aptly demonstrated. Shelby was obviously looking for his approval and Braden smiled and nodded. The corners of the touching little mouth turned up just enough to let Braden know he had received the message. Funny how they were getting so they could talk without words—very like he and his sister had done.

With dinner finished, the ladies retired to the sitting room for coffee, and the children disappeared. As Braden pulled out his pipe and tobacco, he looked about for Shelby, but he was not around. *Kid looked tired. Probably gone to the room,* Braden decided. The talk settled into what the Pony would mean to the development of Virginia City and Carson City and the rumor that the Nevada Territory would be carved out of Utah Territory.

William lighted his pipe and after it was burning nicely, he leaned back and warmed to his favorite subject, the growing prosperity of Carson City and a need for Nevada to be free of the shackles of the Mormons in Salt Lake City. "It's too far away for them to understand our problems or care about them," he said.

The men nodded. "Can't communicate across that desert, and Brigham Young isn't about to journey out here to see for himself," one of them added.

"Now that the Pony is running, it should be much easier to get word back and forth," Braden said.

"Won't help much," William persisted. "We don't see things in the same way. And we certainly can't expect any help if the Indians should go on the warpath. We need to have our own government and control our own destinies."

Normally Braden would have been right in the thick of the discussion, but tonight he couldn't seem to keep his mind on the conversation. His thoughts kept straying to Shelby. You could never tell about kids. Maybe the boy hadn't turned in early after all. Shelby had gawked so when they rode into town, maybe he had decided to go see the sights.

The longer he sat there, the more concerned Braden became. Finally he could sit still no longer. Excusing himself, he left the group. If the kid wasn't in the room, he didn't know what he would do.


Dinner was a nearly unbearable ordeal, and Shelby thought it would never be over. Braden paid her scant attention, devoting himself instead to the raven-haired beauty seated on his right and Elizabeth on his left. He did manage to tear himself away long enough for one quick smile at her, but that was the only acknowledgment he made throughout the entire meal.

*What do you care?* she scolded herself. *He's nothing to you but a kind man who has taken pity on you. You obviously mean nothing to him. Probably wishes he could be rid of you,* she thought as the meal ended and she watched him assist that tall, elegantly-gowned creature to her feet. Braden stood looking deeply into her eyes as she applied her fan with a practiced hand. Shelby wanted to throw things at them both.

*Look at me!* her heart cried to Braden, and she fled from the room before she did some incredibly stupid thing she would regret instantly. She pounded down the long hall, and once inside the room, fell across the bed. Great engulfing sobs rose in spite of everything, and she buried her face in the pillows to absorb the choking sounds which filled the little room.

*Shelby, stop this nonsense!* she commanded herself and with hands doubled into fists beat her frustration into the bed. The tears released only once since Papa's death refused to be stifled, however, and she finally gave in to the cleansing torrent.

At last, having cried herself out, she rose to wash her face. The room was dark, and she fumbled about for a lamp and a match to light it. Why hadn't she been more observant earlier? Her hand hit something solid, and she felt it rock. The thought that she might knock over one of the lovely lamps and break it caused her heart to skip a beat. Braden would have an awful fit if she were so clumsy. Better she should go to bed with a tear-streaked face than raise his wrath.

She stood in front of the dark window as she untied the necktie and folded it neatly. Carson City was too new to have streetlights and if there was a moon, heavy clouds covered it, making the outside as black as the inside of her room. She slipped out of the new boots and wriggled her toes to restore the circulation. She always had disliked breaking in new shoes, and a boy's boots, heavy and unyielding, were worse than anything she had ever experienced.

As she began unbuttoning her shirt, the concern she had suppressed earlier struck with full intensity. There was only one bed, and she was going to have to share it with Braden! She couldn't! She wouldn't! But how was she going to avoid it?

She sat on the chair and with trembling fingers rebuttoned the shirt while her mind tumbled in panic, grasping for a solution. *Face it, Shelby. There's no way out of this, short of leaving.*

She stumbled to the window again and looked out. It

was beginning to snow. Big, heavy flakes spiraled out of the sky and swirled against the window, blocking out the shadowy buildings and turning the world outside into a white-on-black abstract. With no money and no skills, she couldn't leave. She would surely freeze to death without shelter in this new storm.

Returning to the bed, she lay down as near to the edge as she could get. The storm brought with it a rapid drop in temperature, and without a fire in the little stove, the room cooled quickly. Fully clothed, she crept at last under the covers. Although she hung partway off the bed, exhaustion won out, and Shelby fell into a deep dreamless sleep.

Braden felt incredibly foolish as he walked with quiet steps to their room. Kid was probably playing somewhere around the hotel with the younger guests. He'd noticed two or three at dinner. He thought he was foolish to worry over Shelby like he did. Being an instant father was turning into an unexpected burden. He wasn't sure he liked it.

On the off chance Shelby was in the room, he opened the door quietly and held it open so the lamplight from the hall streamed across the bed. There, clutching the edge of the mattress, was the boy.

Braden tiptoed over to have a better look. The kid had hooked one knee over the outside of the bed and was clutching the bedpost with both hands. He was still fully clothed. Only the boots had been removed. The new clothes were a great treat, Braden knew, but to sleep in them?

He bent down to shake Shelby awake. His hand rested on the bony little shoulder, and he looked into the pale face with the skin drawn tightly over fragile bones. Streaks of recent tears stained the cheeks and Braden's heart faltered.

*Poor little kid,* he thought and knelt beside the bed. *He must be terribly frightened, being all alone like he is. Lord, please be with him as he tries to find his way. And guide me to know what's best for him, because he sure needs all the help he can get.*

Braden stayed awhile on his knees, watching the small figure. *Take off those oversized clothes and that face-shielding hat, and Shelby sure is scrawny. He'll have to grow some to amount to anything,* he thought.

Braden had the feeling, however, that Shelby would always be a slight man, and no amount of feed was going to change that. *Probably ought to see he gets some kind of learning so he can make his living in bookkeeping or store clerking—something that doesn't take muscle.*

The temptation to touch the fine skin of Shelby's delicately sculptured face and run his fingers through the soft strands of golden-brown hair nearly overwhelmed Braden, and he rose abruptly. Why lately, every time he came really close to the kid, did he get these strange palpitations of the heart and a smothery feeling in his chest? He started for the door but didn't feel right about leaving the boy hanging three-quarters out of bed. *Couldn't possibly be getting much rest, gripping the handhold so tightly,* he mused to himself.

When Braden tried to uncurl Shelby's fingers, however, he found bands of iron. Even in a sound sleep, Shelby seemed determined not to be moved farther into the bed.

"All right," Braden muttered, giving up. "Stay there, but don't complain in the morning when you're stiff and sore." Annoyed with himself that Shelby mattered so much to him, he quickly left the room.

As Braden entered the lobby, the women were returning from their coffee and he found himself face to face with the beautiful Lila.

"Why, Mr. Russell," Lila purred in a soft drawl. "How nice to run into you. Have the men succeeded so quickly in solving all our problems, both national and local?"

Sapphire blue eyes flashed at him from behind an expertly maneuvered fan.

"Now, Miss Lila, we both know the men only repeat what they hear. It's the women behind the men who find the solutions and whisper them into our ever-listening ears, cleverly making us think the ideas were ours in the first place."

Her eyes shadowed and the smile strained slightly. "What kind of man would ever admit such a thing?"

"An honest one."

"Then obviously we women haven't been as clever as we thought we were, have we?" She didn't seem amused by the discovery.

Braden chuckled. "I don't think your secret is widely known. I must confess I had a sister who betrayed womankind and let me catch a few glimpses of your world."

The wide smile returned and with a charming flip of the raven curls, Lila again became her alluring self. "You had me worried, Mr. Russell. I do feel better knowing you are the exception. If all men were so knowledgeable, it would certainly complicate the system."

She slipped her hand through Braden's arm and guided him to a loveseat in an inconspicuous corner. With practiced charm, she plied him with questions about his background and recent experiences. It had been a long time since he had been the object of such devoted attention by so captivating a woman, and under her spell, Braden felt himself at last beginning to enjoy the evening.

They both started as the large floor clock bonged twelve times. "My goodness, where has the time gone?" Lila said, giving the fan a graceful languorous wave. Then, snapping it shut, she rose. "I apologize for keeping you up. You must be exhausted after all those weeks of discomfort in the desert."

The soft lamplight glowed off the fine skin of her shoulders and throat above the silk gown, carefully chosen to match her eyes.

"I have enjoyed every minute of it," he said. "One doesn't find many women of your cultured background here in the West."

"You're too kind," she said, coyly ducking her head and flashing those fantastic eyes at him from behind the fan once more seductively spread.

Braden took her arm and together they walked slowly across the lobby. At the foot of the stairs, she paused and laid the closed fan across fashionably low-cut ruffles. Braden's eyes followed.

"Elizabeth says you're having to share a bed with the little boy you found. A big man like you ought not to be asked to endure such an inconvenience." Her eyes were wide and innocent. "I have an extra bed going unused in my room."

A rush of heat swept through Braden and he gripped the banister. "Thank you for the offer," he said, keeping his voice cool.

But he was thanking God for the months of practice in showing no emotion, for he had the greatest urge to slap her. Why would Elizabeth allow such a woman to mingle with respectable ladies? Surely she had no suspicion of Lila's profession.

"Shelby and I shall manage just fine, ma'am. He's not very big and takes very little room." Braden gave Lila a curt nod. "Good night." He wheeled from her and if it hadn't been so late, would have stomped out his anger down the hall.

However, out of consideration for the other guests, he was forced to walk softly the length of the hall. As he opened the door to his room, he turned and found Lila still standing, posed on the stairs under one of the lamps, watching him expectantly. *No, Lila, I'm not going to change my mind,* he thought and grimly shut the door behind him.

Snow had plastered the window white and the room was like a cave. Giving Lila time to get upstairs, Braden opened the door to permit enough light to find the lamp. Having struck a white phosphorous match and coughed at the fumes, he lit the wick, careful to keep the flame low. Shelby lay as he had left her, still clutching the bedpost and curled over the edge of the bed.

He carried the lamp to the bedside table and lowered his big frame onto the bed. It creaked its objection to his weight, and Shelby gave a little cry.

Turning to look at him, Braden said softly, "It's all right, kid. Nobody's going to hurt you. They'll have to get past me first." He took off his boots and set them neatly by the bed. The light picked up Shelby's shiny new boots set in a pair by the dresser and the carefully folded tie lying on top. *Funny kid. Sometimes he's neat as a girl. Then, just when you think he's trained, he up and makes pigs look clean.*

Braden stretched out on top of the covers and laced his fingers behind his head. He tried to relax, but that crazy kid hanging off the bed was driving him wild. He knew just as soon as he got to sleep, Shelby would loosen his grip and hit the floor in a crashing heap.

Finally Braden could stand it no longer. "Shelby," he said in a low firm voice. "Get on this bed!" He didn't move.

Braden watched a minute longer, then reached up and jerked the boy's hand free from the bedpost. He threw back the covers and grabbed Shelby by the belt, hoisting him onto the bed. There was a slight moan as the little body curled into a ball and a hand groped for covers. Braden gently pulled the quilts up and carefully tucked them under Shelby's chin. The hand reappeared and slid beneath the cheek resting against the pillow.

The lamplight dancing against the walls cast deep flickering shadows about the room. Braden lay staring at Shelby. Gradually the tense posture relaxed and he turned over to face Braden, straightening his body into a normal sleeping position. The weary lines in his face disappeared and a peace descended over the features that Braden hadn't seen since they'd met. The thick lashes made dark smudges under Shelby's eyes, and the hair fell around his face, softening the too-thin features.

It seemed Braden couldn't get his fill of looking at the kid. *What a crazy feeling*, he thought. Like nothing he had experienced before. This being a parent was all right.

Even through his clothes he began to feel the penetrating cold, so Braden slid beneath the first layer of quilts. With the light still on, he continued to gaze at the boy until Braden, too, went to sleep, carrying the image of the peaceful face with him.

## CHAPTER 10

WHEN SHELBY WOKE IN THE MORNING, she found herself alone in the room. Where was Braden? Several ideas crossed her mind until she remembered Lila. Well, Shelby didn't blame him. Lila was certainly a better alternative than sharing a bed with a boy. Nevertheless, the thought brought with it the threat of tears. It hurt to think Braden might be that kind of man.

Slowly Shelby laid back the covers and let her feet dangle over the edge of the bed. The window, viewless through its coat of frozen snow, allowed a filtered blue-white light into the frigid room. Wasting no time or motion, Shelby quickly washed and dressed in her new workclothes.

Straightening from the tussle with the second boot, she started at the soft knock on the door. What could Henry want at this hour? Perhaps he was sent to waken her. The knock came again, a bit louder this time.

She swung the door open. "C—come in," she stammered.

Braden, still in his dinner clothes now rumpled and twisted, marched through, his arms laden with clothes and boots. Throwing the stack of new garments on the bed, he sat down in the chair, twisting and rubbing his neck as he did so.

He had to have spent the night in an uncomfortable position, and his mood was reminiscent of an old bull deprived of his favorite pasture. "Where you been?" she asked, moving to the far side of the room near the window.

He scowled at her through bloodshot eyes. "When a person hogs the bed and refuses to be budged, it doesn't leave a certain other person any choice but to make different arrangements."

"I'm sorry," she said, hanging her head. "Where did you end up spending the night?"

"In the reading room. And after trying all of them, I can testify there are *no* comfortable chairs to be had. I don't know how those old fellows can doze in them all day."

"They're a lot shorter'n you. Makes a difference, you know."

"H'm," he murmured as he stripped off the thoroughly mussed shirt and poured water in the basin. "Weather's turned cold again. You need to go to the store and buy a coat. Charge it on my account. Right after breakfast we're going to see Bolivar Roberts about a job for you."

Shelby, grateful to escape, mumbled an awkward thanks, dashed out the door and down the hall to the dining room.

When Braden joined her at the table, he appeared somewhat mollified, but shadows still darkened his countenance. Fortunately everyone up at this hour preferred his own company, and the only sounds around the table were the clinking of china and utensils.

At a crisp rustle, Shelby looked up to see the Ormsbys entering the dining room. Major Ormsby scanned the table until his eyes rested on Braden.

"Must have been some night," the Major said with a wink.

"Yeah," Braden growled. "Kid took the whole bed and refused to move. By the way, your reading room needs a couch."

Elizabeth's eyes widened. "I shall see that you have a

bed tonight, even if I have to set up a cot in the hall for Shelby," she said, sitting in the empty place next to Braden.

*That will be fine with me,* Shelby thought, grateful to know she wouldn't have to devise some scheme to escape sharing Braden's bed. Noticing she had finished, Braden waved her in the direction of the store, and he hunched over another cup of coffee, letting the conversation lapse.

It didn't take Shelby long to choose a heavy gray mackinaw and a black knit cap which tied firmly over her ears. She was just pulling on woolen mittens when Braden joined her.

"Thought I'd better come in and see about your choices." He turned her around. "Not bad, kid."

*I've been choosing my own clothes for a number of years, Father,* she thought as she subjected herself to his scrutiny. Braden, finding a coat for himself similar to hers, signed the bill and hurried her out into the snow-drifted street. They slipped and slid their way to the Russell, Majors, and Waddell freight station.

At their entrance, a broad-shouldered, well-dressed man of about forty, his feet propped on the scarred desk top, looked up at them over the newspaper he was reading. A smile lit his face and he quickly swung fifty-dollar boots to the floor.

"Braden Russell, you old scoundrel! Good to see you, feller!" His voice vibrated with enthusiasm as he came, hand extended, to greet Braden.

Only after the two men concluded their detailed discussion of the Pony's progress, did Braden make mention of Shelby.

"By the way," he began casually as though this were a very recent idea. "Ran into this kid on the trail. Make a good hostler if you've a need for one."

Bolivar Roberts turned intense deep-set eyes on Shelby. She felt he could see right through her, and she shriveled under his scrutiny.

"Not very big, is he?"

"No, but he's strong and a good worker." Braden

placed a possessive hand on her shoulder and told how she had cared for the lathered horse at Buckland's.

Bolivar, never taking his eyes from her, rubbed his chin as though this act helped in decision making. When Braden finished talking, only the ticking of the clock and the cheerful crackling fire interrupted the silence of the room. Braden slowly pivoted her around as Bolivar weighed his decision.

Shelby felt as if she were the entry at a horse auction and the buyer wasn't sure she was worth the price. *Want to look at my teeth?*

When Shelby thought she couldn't stand being the focus of both men another second, Bolivar Roberts nodded.

"Since he already knows the ropes at Buckland's, let's send him back there. Sam'll see he's taken care of, and I can fire that useless piece of skin that hasn't been doing the job. What's your name?" he said, nudging Shelby.

Shelby, having scarcely spoken this morning, started to answer him, but her voice cracked in a funny high squeak. Both men laughed.

"He's that age, all right," Bolivar said.

She blushed and cleared her throat. "Shelby Jackson, Mr. Roberts, sir."

"Nice to meet you, Shelby Jackson." He shook her hand and pointed to his desk. "If you'll step over here, we'll sign you up and swear you in as an official employee of the Pony Express."

Braden slouched into a barrel chair near the tall heating stove but kept an eye on Shelby.

Bolivar returned to his desk and began leafing through the papers stacked there. "How long would you push a pony at top speed?" he asked as he continued to shuffle papers.

She gulped. This wasn't what she had expected. "I don't guess more'n an hour, tops. At that, only if the conditions we—was right."

He merely nodded, scrambling the once-neat stacks. "What would you do if you met Indians on the trail?"

The scene at the mine flashed into her mind and Shelby

bit her lip. "I'd get me and my pony away, quick as I could."

"You wouldn't try to fight them?"

*Now, here goes the job,* she thought dismally. "No sir," she said in a steady voice. "Even two or three would be too many for me. Could get me killed and the pony stole. Mr. Russell says you paid a good price for the ponies. Don't guess you'd take kindly to them getting thieved." *Could always hire another hostler, though.*

"What's your first responsibility?" He laid aside a dog-eared sheet and began straightening the mess his search had created.

"The mail, sir. Always. That's what the Pony's all about. Gettin' the mail through . . . and on time."

He looked over at Braden. "You've done a good job, Russell. The boy here knows his stuff. Mail first, horses second. Everything else, last." He grinned at Shelby. "I'm proud to swear you in as a member of the Pony. Hold up your right hand."

Shelby swelled with delight. "Yes, sir!"

"Repeat after me, 'I hereby swear before the great living God that during my engagement and while I am an employee of Russell, Majors, and Waddell, I will under no circumstance use profane language; that I will drink no intoxicating liquors; that I will not quarrel or fight with other employees of the firm, and that I will conduct myself honestly, be faithful to my duties, and so direct my acts as to win the confidence of my employers, so help me God.'"

"So help me God," Braden echoed.

Bolivar turned to him. "What was that all about?"

"I've been an employee of the Pony for several weeks. Didn't know I was supposed to take an oath. Thought I'd rectify the oversight."

"You want a Bible, too?" Bolivar asked as he handed Shelby a red leather-covered copy. "Majors bought a supply of these specially bound Bibles for the wagon-train crews. We've been instructed to use them up."

It was the loveliest Bible Shelby had ever owned, and she wanted to clasp it to her chest. However, she didn't think boys did things like that, so she imitated Braden's actions. He ran his hand over the soft leather and leafed through the pages.

She watched his eyes come to rest on the Ninety-first Psalm. It seemed she could follow him as he read of the Lord's saving power when man's strength was quite gone. Read of God offering security as He promised to "cover thee with his feathers and his wings shalt thou trust . . ." Shelby read the entire Psalm, feeling that its message was just for her.

Then she looked again at Braden and there was an unfamiliar twisting of his face as if he were fighting a great and painful war inside. She knew a deep hurt remained unhealed. A hurt from a battle that flogged him ceaselessly. She prayed the forces of God would win.

His hands shook as he reverently closed the beautiful book. "Thanks," Braden said, a slight tremor in his voice.

"How soon can you have Shelby out to Buckland's?" Bolivar asked.

Quickly recovering his poise, Braden answered briskly, "We can ride out today."

"Good. Do it. The westbound rider is due and several freight wagons will need tending to." Turning to Shelby, he held out his hand. "Glad to have you working for us. Something you'll never forget, I promise you."

"Thank you, sir," Shelby replied.

In silence, they made their way back to the Ormsby House. Shelby clutched the Bible, her mind dwelling on the Scripture she and Braden had shared. She noticed he, too, held tightly to his Bible.

They stomped the snow from their boots and entered the lobby. Except for Mr. Chandler tending his tobacco shop in the corner, the room was empty.

"Want to catch up on the latest news in the reading room before we leave?" Braden asked. "They have a fine selection of newspapers from both west and east."

Shelby nodded and followed him into the quiet light-filled room. Braden selected two high-backed wing chairs arranged for privacy in a corner. Unbuttoning their coats, they claimed their spots and Braden rattled a San Francisco newspaper into submission.

Shelby opened her Bible to the psalm she had read earlier and slowly read it again. The security offered in the words seemed just what she needed. While she had tried not to harden her heart against Papa's killers, she hadn't been entirely successful. There was a stonelike lump in her breast, and she knew she hadn't been fully forgiving.

Now, as she read, she realized perhaps her faith that the killers would receive their full punishment in the Lord's own good time hadn't been particularly strong. The words blurred before her eyes as she pondered the blessings promised by the Lord. His promise of guidance, of victory, and fellowship began to take on new meaning.

"Kid?" Braden's voice, though soft in deference to others in the room, was nevertheless jarring.

It was only when she tried to focus her eyes on him that she became aware of her tears. Hastily she wiped them from her cheeks with the back of her hand.

He folded the paper and laid it in his lap. "How about telling me what's troubling you?"

Shelby's emotions tumbled out of control, and all she could do was shake her head and mop at the tears now cascading onto the front of her shirt.

Unfolding a new handkerchief, Braden handed it to her. "Shelby, talk to me," he ordered, the concern growing in his eyes.

It took some time before she could regain control, but he waited patiently. "Didn't mean to cry like a sissy," she snubbed, wiping her hand across her eyes.

"Been wondering when you would. It's not good to keep the grief over your pa bottled up inside. Needs to come out and get settled."

Silence, teeming with their own thoughts, lay heavy between them.

Shelby looked deeply into his lusterless eyes. "I'd say you had something hid inside you, too," she said, gasping inwardly at her boldness.

Braden dropped his eyes and studied the backs of his clasped hands. "Thought I was getting real good at keeping my feelings hidden," he said at last.

"Oh, you are. But that's a giveaway, too."

Slowly, in bits and pieces, Braden told her of his father's abuse at the hands of the stagecoach robbers and the death of his beloved sister. His voice was devoid of any emotion, its coldness sending shivers through Shelby. "And when I find those who murdered her, I'm going to see they die—slow and painful."

In her shock over his statement, Shelby forgot the role she was playing. "You have no right to mete out justice. Vengeance is the Lord's and punishment for such crimes as you have described is for the law. When you stoop to such an act, you become no better than those who committed them against you and yours."

Braden glared at her, but instead of backing down, she returned his cold hard stare.

"Those are extremely weighty words for a fifteen-year-old," he said, eyeing her with a curious look.

"Uh," Shelby shifted nervously from one foot to the other. "My Aunt Hally said things like that a lot. Guess they just got inside and stuck. Didn't know what she was sayin' at the time. But now I got my own battle against wantin' to get even, and I'm beginnin' to understand it some."

Braden sank back into the chair and idly reached for his Bible. Shelby watched as he let it fall open and began to read. His forehead creased with the intensity of his study.

Finally he raised stricken eyes to hers. "I can't make any meaning out of the words. I repeat the verse, but it makes no sense."

"Aunt Hally always said if your heart wasn't pure, the Word of God couldn't live there. If you don't know the Lord, you can't understand his Word. It's through his Spirit that we know his teachin's."

"Did Aunt Hally also say how one gets a pure heart?"

Shelby caught the hard, sarcastic note which crept into his voice, but she chose to ignore it. "By repentin' of the desire to get even. You got a bigger job, 'cause you don't only want to get even, you want to do worse."

Braden glared at her and slammed the Bible shut. "You bet I do. There's no law out here even cares about my sister's killers. I'm the only one to do it."

"If you'll give Him a chance, the Lord will see justice done."

"Did it occur to you that he might be using me for that purpose?" Braden's voice had turned to steel, cold and unyielding.

"If he is, why do you feel so terrible? When I do God's will, I know it because I get a warm feelin' around my heart." She cocked her head and looked at him.

He must surely be suspicious of her by now, but his salvation was more important than her continuing deception and the promise of the best paying employment to be had. For the first time since Papa's death, she stopped fretting about trying to run her life and placed her future in the Lord's hands. She wasn't going to worry about what would become of her anymore. And with that decision, the wonderful warm feeling she had just described to Braden infused her being. *Thank you Lord,* she prayed.

Suddenly Braden sprang out of his chair, nearly overturning it in his haste. He threw a paper onto the table and stalked from the room without a backward glance. Shelby rushed after him, but even though she ran, she failed to catch him until he paused to unlock the door of their room.

"Get your things together. We're leaving," he said, his voice harsh and unrecognizable.

110

## CHAPTER 11

As soon as SHELBY AND BRADEN could get their horses wrangled and saddled and their new clothes stuffed into saddlebags, they were off. Even Elizabeth's most persuasive words, Major Ormsby's dire predictions about the weather, and Lila's flawless fan technique did nothing to deter Braden's determined and hasty departure.

Shelby looked at the pewter sky and drew her coat tighter about her. "Wind sure is cold," she commented as they cantered into the desert.

"Be grateful. This time it's at your back, and you have warm clothes," Braden growled.

*So much for conversation,* Shelby thought and retreated into a silence which lasted until they were in sight of the lights at Buckland's.

Shelby was starving, for they had brought nothing with them and Braden had refused to stop at any of the stations along the way.

After leading their tired animals into the corral, Shelby unsaddled them for the night. She found the grain and gave them each a coffee can full while Braden went inside to make Sam Buckland aware of his new hostler.

When Shelby entered the smoke-filled room, she

immediately felt Sam's eyes on her, pinning her to the spot where she stood. She didn't dare look up, but she felt the intensity of his gaze as he walked over to her.

Sam grasped her chin and tilted her head until she was forced to look at him. "Not much substance here," he said in an ominous voice.

"Kid's not big, but he's strong," Braden spoke in her defense. "He's the one who took care of the mustang the night of the first Pony ride, remember?"

Sam didn't take his eyes from Shelby. "Don't remember who did the job. Know it wasn't the one hired to do it. Found him drunk behind the grain in the tack room."

Braden came to stand next to her. "Besides, being small, the kid'll make a good relief rider in case of trouble."

Sam took his fingers from her chin. In deliberate movements he folded his arms across his chest and stared at her. "Dunno . . . just don't have the right feeling about him."

Shelby's heart dropped into her shoes. How could he possibly suspect? She hadn't spoken a word, so it couldn't be her voice, and in the new clothes, she looked more like a boy than ever.

"How much did Roberts say to pay him?" Sam asked.

Shelby gulped. Now that she thought back, the amount hadn't been discussed. She had left all that to Braden.

"When I told Roberts how Shelby had taken care of the horse, he said the kid didn't need breaking in. Plans to start him at thirty dollars a month," Braden said.

Sam shook his head. "Too much for a scrawny little customer like that. Roberts see him?"

"Swore him in and gave him a Bible."

"Well, kid, for that kind of money, you're going to work like you never worked before." Sam's eyes took on a menacing glitter as he wheeled and stalked back behind the bar.

Shelby cringed. Maybe that look was why the other poor hostler had gotten drunk and hidden. Suddenly Shelby had great sympathy for the fellow. A comforting arm came to rest around her shoulder, and she looked up into Braden's face.

"Don't let Sam scare you. He looks ferocious, but he's a fair man to work for. You do your job right and you'll have no trouble with him." As he spoke Braden piloted her to a small table against the far wall in time to receive heaping bowls of hot stew.

Shelby removed her new gloves and jammed them into her jacket pocket. She would have liked to wash her hands, but that would definitely arouse suspicion. With the cap still tied and her coat only unbuttoned, she dived into the steaming bowl in front of her and didn't come up for air until she could see the bottom. Then she took a piece of sourdough bread, sopped up the last of the succulent gravy clinging to the tin bowl, and washed down the dry crust with a drink of water.

"Enough?" Braden asked.

Wiping her mouth with the back of her hand, she nodded.

"You sleep over in that corner." Braden inclined his head in the general direction.

Shelby's eyes followed his look to the corner near the fireplace where a tumbled pile of quilts gave hint of a bed. All she could think of was the lice which surely inhabited so cozy a place. Her head began itching at the thought of crawling under that bedding.

"You don't look too happy with the sleeping arrangements."

"Can't help wonderin' how many and what kind of folks have slept there since the covers were last washed."

"Getting awfully picky since your stay at the Ormsby House, aren't you?" Braden's voice held a hard edge.

"Don't relish lice for company," she shot at him, trying to make her voice surly.

"I'd guess Sam's had that stuff washed and aired. Don't reckon he's too fond of lice in his own head of hair, either."

Shelby breathed a sigh of relief.

Braden pulled on his gloves. "Well, good luck, kid. Do what Sam tells you and stay out of his way the rest of the time. You'll make out fine." There was an unusual gruff quality in his voice.

Though she tried to look into his eyes, Braden kept his face averted as he walked toward the door. A rush of panic surged over Shelby when she realized he was in the process of leaving. She dashed to his side.

"Why'd you unsaddle your horse if you're goin' tonight? Besides, it's not safe to ride alone." Her words tumbled over each other as she tried to formulate reasons why he should stay.

He buttoned his coat and pushed his hat low over his eyes. "I'm taking a fresh horse. And who said it wasn't safe?"

Shelby waved her hands in a feeble gesture. "Well, uh, nobody today. Just keep hearin' it. You remember the talk in Carson City about the Indians? Doesn't that scare you?" Though she knew he must leave eventually, she was grasping at straws now—anything to postpone the parting.

"Nope." Taking his pistol from its holster, he spun the cylinder and with a nod of satisfaction, replaced it on his hip. "See you around, kid. I'll get back as often as I can."

Without a backward glance, Braden disappeared out the door. And though he didn't know it, he was taking Shelby's heart with him.

Soon the days settled into a routine. Once a week two riders came through, one going east and one west. Since this was a home station, the riders lived here; however, Sam kept Shelby so busy she had little time to visit with the men when they were off duty.

Since Sam's place was also on the freight line, Shelby cared for the mule teams as well as the Pony mustangs. When she wasn't looking after livestock, Sam had her wiping tables and washing dishes in the saloon. No matter that it wasn't Pony business. He was determined she was going to earn her thirty dollars a month, even if he had to keep her busy working for him.

Shelby soon realized that when she was through tending the animals, she'd better make herself scarce, or she'd end up working eighteen hours a day! Once she learned the freight and Pony schedules and had performed the necessary rituals in the care of the mules and horses, Shelby began stealing an hour or two to explore the nearby countryside.

She did such a conscientious job of tending to the sores and cuts of the animals in her care and making sure the Pony horses were thoroughly cooled down before leaving them that Sam ignored her presence more and more, giving her longer periods of free time. This she used to hike and explore.

April, however, was a cruel month. The snow fell, melted, then repeated the pattern until the ground was hard with ice in the morning, slippery with mud by noon, and frozen over once again in the evening. Even in her new coat, the bone-chilling wind, called the Washoe Zephyr, whipped across the landscape in a steady scream and turned Buckland's Station into raw freezing punishment which spared no one. It knifed through Shelby, making her work outside a constant misery. Yet even so, it was preferable to the odor-laden air and crowded conditions inside the station.

Many days she wondered if the money was worth the bleeding lips and hands. Braden didn't return, and Shelby began to feel trapped in this untamed inhospitable land with its unrelenting winds and snows. The stories told around the card tables in the evening were horrifying—stories of terrible heat, dust, and death.

So April passed and May arrived. The Pony runs settled into a routine broken only when the weather slowed the western rider over the Sierras. Even by the first of May, winter had not yet released its icy hold. But travelers and freight drivers spoke of warmer days, of gold and silver strikes in the Comstock Lode that helped to make all the suffering worthwhile.

Shelby claimed herself a horse, one the Pony had ridden too hard and too far. Sam had instructed her to cut out the little beast and he would put it out of its misery. However, Shelby knew that with proper care, the sturdy animal would make a good pony for easy trips, and she was determined to save it.

Since she worked not only for the Pony but also for Sam, he allowed her free use of his bridge. She rode across the Carson River and turned east along the stream, swift and mud-clogged from the spring runoff.

The air began to cool rapidly as the sun dropped low in the western sky, and the temperature change wakened Shelby from a peaceful nap atop a warm flat rock. It was the first really undisturbed sleep she had had in months, and she felt greatly refreshed. Having found the pony grazing contentedly not far away, she tightened the cinch on the saddle, and though some distance from the river, she rode down for a drink. As her horse climbed onto the rise above the Carson River Narrows, a thin line of riders from east across the river caught her attention.

Quickly she moved away from the skyline, dismounted, and tied the pony to a bush. "Thank goodness, I thought to bring these field glasses," she said aloud as she raised them to her eyes. Her hand began to shake slightly as she saw nine Indians riding single file into the river bottomland below her.

Slipping behind some protective rocks, Shelby continued to watch as the grim-faced men rode into a grove of cottonwoods near the river and picketed their ponies. Then, on foot, they quietly climbed the high knoll overlooking the river, and for the first time Shelby recognized her exact location.

It was almost sundown as the Indians approached the Williams brothers' log station on the California Trail. From her vantage point on high ground, she could see a covered wagon standing in the yard and a slender spiral of smoke drifting lazily from the chimney.

Four men stepped from the station and stretched in the clear air, then one climbed into the wagon. The others draped themselves over the wagonbox to continue their visit, until one of them spotted the Indians.

Through the glasses, Shelby watched the man drop down from the wagon and the four of them, fear etching their faces, seemed frozen to the spot as the Indians surrounded them. Shelby was too far away to hear what was being said, but she had no difficulty in understanding that the Williams brothers were desperately trying to talk their way out of a dangerous situation.

The leader of the Indians, an imposing figure with his arms crossed over his chest, stared at the men, now gesticulating wildly. The warriors listened impassively to the white men's talk, but kept a cautious eye on the four who were pacing with short, impatient steps, casting about for some avenue of escape.

Then all at once, one of the station keepers cut away from the circle of Indians and began running west in the direction of Buckland's. Two warriors gave chase and caught him easily, dragging him to stand again with the other terrified whites.

Shelby found she was unconsciously praying for some intervention in the situation, which was rapidly growing serious. She thought of riding for help, but in this open country she would surely be spotted and seized at once.

The faces of the men at the station had drained of color, but they continued talking as they grew more and more agitated. There was much pointing toward the barn and shaking of heads.

Scanning each of the Indians, Shelby noticed a fresh ugly scar on the leg of one of the braves and recognized the young warrior she'd seen the day she and Braden had come through Williams' Station.

The white men were nearly hysterical. Shelby felt a sudden wave of nausea, but she was riveted to the drama unfolding before her.

The Indians continued to stand, keeping a quiet vigil. Finally, apparently unable to bear the suspense any longer, another of the station tenders broke away. He ran toward the bluff, jumped, and rolled until he reached the river, with the warriors in swift pursuit. The man hesitated only briefly before plunging into the icy current of the Carson River. He flailed away frantically, trying to swim, but he couldn't keep his head above the rushing water. He went under, came up and gasped for air, and went down again. The swift water carried his body downstream and into an eddy. The Indians pulled him ashore, carried him up the bluff, and deposited him inside the station.

Upon seeing his unconscious companion, one of the three remaining men shouted at his captors, drew his long-bladed hunting knife and tried to fight his way toward the corral where fresh horses for the Pony were kept. Some of the Indians grabbed his knife-wielding arm and yanked it upward behind his back. The knife spun away into the white alkali dirt. As the circle closed tightly around the white men, Shelby squeezed her eyes shut and lowered the glasses. She didn't want to see more.

When Shelby finally found courage to look again, three bodies lay strewn in the yard, and the warriors were emerging from the barn with two sobbing Indian girls. Shelby guessed their ages to be near twelve or thirteen. The girls were placed on horses from the corral and led from the knoll to where the Indian ponies were picketed.

The remaining warriors gathered the bodies of the dead and carried them into the cabin, then lit bunches of dried grass to form blazing torches.

With Williams' Station afire, the Indians walked back to the river bottom and into the trees where their horses were staked. Here, they could not only watch the fiery destruction of the cabin, but could command an excellent view of the surrounding countryside.

Shelby forced down her rising panic and remained crouched out of sight behind the large rock. If the angry Indians spotted her, she would be as dead as the Williams brothers.

A Paiute rider left immediately, retracing the trail along which they had ridden, but the rest of the party made camp.

Shelby, being unfamiliar with the terrain, dared not try riding back to Buckland's in the dark, and became an unwilling, if unknown, prisoner of the group of warriors lounging in the trees.

She unsaddled her horse and tied him to graze, praying he would not catch the scent of the horses across the river. One nicker and she would be a dead woman.

Although Shelby found a burrow under a large sagebrush, the night was too cold and she was too frightened to sleep. She feared, too, that Sam Buckland, who took seriously Braden's admonition to keep a close eye on her, would come looking for her and stumble upon the sleeping Indians.

Then it occurred to her that Braden might choose this time to return for a visit, and she grew almost hysterical at the thought of his riding innocently through the grove of trees. Though straining to see into the shadows illuminated by sporadic beams of moonlight, Shelby could not make out the exact whereabouts of the Indians.

When, a couple of hours before dawn, she heard the party leave with no further incident, she offered up a prayer of gratitude.

Shortly after the departure of the Indians, she heard the swift gallop of two horses and knew it was the westbound Pony rider, J.B. Bartoles, with a mounted escort or maybe a companion. With clouds covering the moon, she could only surmise the moment they came to the burned-out cabin. Then there were the sounds of fresh horses being saddled and the thud of hooves as the riders made for Buckland's with the news.

At the first light in the eastern sky, Shelby caught her horse and followed as quickly as the disabled animal could stand. All the while she traveled, she carefully ordered the details of what she had seen so as to give an accurate description.

Shelby needn't have bothered, however, for the people at Buckland's were clustered tightly around someone when she arrived, and no one even noticed her ride over the bridge, unsaddle her horse, and turn him in with the rest of the stock in the corral. The Pony riders, nowhere in sight, must have delivered their message and then ridden on to Carson City to deliver the news personally to Bolivar Roberts.

Elbowing her way into the crowd, Shelby was astonished to hear a man telling a fantastic story about escaping from five hundred crazed Indians on horseback.

119

In a piercing voice, still quaking with the terror he described, he told of the fearsome scene of unprovoked murder, burning, and finally the Indians' pursuit of him as he managed to get a pony and make good his escape to Buckland's.

He told how he'd risked his own life to warn the innocent souls in two cabins on the opposite side of the river from Williams' Station. But it was too late. The doors to their cabins stood ajar, and though he had called loudly at close range, there was no sign of life. The unholy murdering wretches had surely killed at least a dozen or more helpless men, women, and children.

When he was finished, a battle cry, fueled by his terrifying tale, roared up from his audience.

Shelby pushed her way through the group until she stood near the speaker whom she recognized as James Williams, the man who had so angered Braden on their last visit. He was now adding lurid details to his story. Sam had to be told the truth.

Spotting the burly stationmaster across the room, she shoved through the crowd until she reached him. But Sam was listening with rapt attention and would not be distracted.

When she pulled on his jacket sleeve, he pushed her aside. "Take care of Jim's horse," he ordered. "Can't you see I'm busy?"

"But Sam . . ." Shelby pursued.

"But *nothing*. Shut up and do what I say."

With that, he turned back to the tall tale spinning from the evil-looking mouth, leaving Shelby with no alternative but to do as she was told.

*Dear Lord, what am I going to do? That man is going to bring a terrible and unjust retaliation to the Indians who were only trying to rescue their little girls from being sold as slaves. Please, please do something,* she pleaded as she watered and fed the lathered horse. If Braden would only come, he would listen to her and then talk some sense into those who were already threatening revenge for what they believed was a wanton act of murder.

She slipped back inside just as Williams led the way into the saloon.

"First round of drinks is on me!" he called back over his shoulder.

The crowd lined up, elbow to elbow, spanning the entire length of the bar. Sam made his way to the other side and began pouring whiskey as fast as he could set out glasses. The tables quickly filled until there was only room to lounge along the walls. Still they came, listening as the tale was told and retold, growing even bloodier with each retelling.

Then, as fear gripped them, nobody waited for clean glasses. They grabbed the bottles and gulped the raw stuff, increasing their frenzy. Shouts of vindication rang out, and the air was thick with hatred. It seemed as if it were a tangible thing, following the smoke rising to the ceiling and floating in streamers around the hanging lamps.

To escape the drunken panic, Shelby crept into the tack room. Shivering, she curled up behind the grain sacks.

"Braden," she whispered into the blackness, "please come. I'm so frightened and lonesome. I need you."

Exhausted from the lack of sleep the evening before and the emotional strain of the scene she had just witnessed, Shelby fell into a deep slumber, leaving behind her burdens for a few welcome hours.

## CHAPTER 12

DAZED, SHELBY LOOKED UP into Sam's angry face. Rough hands were shaking her awake. Even in the sliver of light from the nearly closed door, she could see his eyes blaze in anger and his whole body tremble with his fury. She pulled herself into a tight ball as far from his grasping hand as the limited space allowed.

"So this is where you disappeared to!" he yelled. "I've even asked some of the boys to hunt for you." Leaning far over the grain sacks, he grabbed the first thing he could get his hands on, her hair. Yanking Shelby to her feet, he shook her like a rag doll. "Got enough problems right now," he thundered. "I don't need you to act up!" He paused, thrust his face into hers and sniffed. "You been drinkin'?" he asked.

"N—no," Shelby stammered when he finally stopped jerking her about and she could find her voice. "Guess some liquor spilled on me."

He shoved her against the grain sacks, and still holding her by the hair of her head, twisted her shirt front with his other hand.

"You'd better not start! Braden Russell'd skin your hide and sell it for shoe leather if he wuz to learn you'd drunk hard liquor at your age."

Sam stared at Shelby with terrifying intensity as though trying to drive his anger deep inside her. Still breathing hard from the exertion, he let her go at last.

Shelby sank against the stacked grain. Reaching trembling fingers to her head, she gingerly felt to see if she were bald. Other than a sore scalp, everything seemed to be in place.

Sam pointed toward the saloon and stabbed the air with his index finger. "Place is full. Folks is gatherin' here for protection against them murderin' savages. I need your help." Though he again breathed normally, his voice was hoarse and cracked as he spoke.

Pushing the door open wide, Sam allowed a large rectangle of light to illumine the tack room. Shelby looked closely at him. Even in the soft glow, his face appeared drawn, and his eyes, ringed with dark circles, sank even farther than usual into his head. Suddenly it dawned on her that perhaps his mistreatment of her had been brought about by exhaustion and fear for her safety.

"I'm sorry I caused you worry, Sam," she said in a soft voice. "The place was so crowded and noisy, I didn't think I could get any sleep."

The relief on his face spoke volumes. "That's a mighty lame excuse for sneakin' off when I was busier'n a hound dog with fleas," he said, his voice still gruff. Then he stalked away.

"Sam, I need to tell you what I saw yesterday at Williams' Station," she began as she followed on his heels.

He paused in the doorway and cut her short. "Don't lie to me, kid. Nobody but Jim was close enough to see what happened . . . and lived to tell it." He narrowed his eyes, scrutinizing her closely. "I can understand your thinkin' you were there—what with all the talk goin' on. But I'll forget you brought it up, 'long as you don't mention it again." He snaked out a long thin arm, whirled her about, and pushed her in front of him into the fetid air of the saloon.

The place was packed with drunken, bragging men—men drinking courage from the bottles they waved in the air as they swore vengeance on the cowardly savages who had murdered those fine Williams's brothers. Tired women and frightened children huddled in corners or leaned against the walls, seeking to shut out the noise and horror.

Shelby dived behind the bar, away from Sam's bony fingers. Seeing some empty water buckets, she grabbed them and fled outside into the moonlit night. Halfway to the river, she heard Sam's voice bawling after her.

"Shelby Jackson, get back in here, unless you've lost all fondness for your hair."

What was the matter with him? Nothing was going to happen. It took her a second to realize Sam didn't know that. "I'll be all right," she called over his shoulder, and despite his profane stream of threats, she raced on to the river.

The next three days were filled with an unending round of hysterical tales told by frightened travelers. Though deeply concerned for Braden. Shelby allowed only a random thought of him to surface. If she once gave in to her fears for his safety, her vivid imagination would run amok and she wasn't sure she could bring it back under control. There was enough panic. A few reasonably calm minds were necessary to keep the station functioning.

On the second day after the Williams' Station massacre, the liquor ran out, and the men at Buckland's were forced to sober up and face the reality of an imminent Indian attack. Terrified souls, including freight drivers, straggled in to Sam's place as they fled the rampaging Indians farther west. They told of harrassment and escape, of the burning of the Pony stations, and the gathering of a volunteer army from Genoa, Carson City, and Virginia City, commanded by Major Ormsby.

Finally Shelby could no longer ignore the gruesome stories. Knowing Braden might be in serious trouble that even he could not handle, she was forced to acknowledge how much she really cared for him and began asking the new arrivals if they had seen or heard of Braden Russell. But no one had any word.

Unable to endure the idea that he might be one of the victims described in such macabre detail, she prayed constantly that he was in the eastern desert, safe from the violence that was building, threatening to erupt into a full-scale war at any moment.

On the tenth of May, an advance rider informed Sam he could expect the army to arrive and camp at his station by afternoon.

At this news Shelby felt the strength drain from her knees. Would Braden be coming with the army? Had he even heard of the beginning of the war? Or, would her worst fears be realized—had he already fallen victim to an Indian tomahawk? Her fertile imagination was well-sown with horror stories told by those who had seen the incidents firsthand, stories embroidered in the retelling at Buckland's Station. In spite of what she knew to be the truth, a falsehood, if believed and acted upon, could produce the same chilling effect.

All morning, as she tended the horses and mules, Shelby kept her eyes glued to the west. It had been over a month since she had seen Braden. If, when he arrived, he was too busy with his duties to pay her any attention, it would be enough simply to watch him. Watch the determined way he moved in long smooth strides. Watch the muscles in his broad shoulders flex as he hoisted his saddle and carried it one-handed to a waiting fence rail. Watch the corners of his mouth twitch slightly before spreading slowly into a smile—a smile that never reached his eyes. Now that she knew what lay in his heart, though, she understood the unfeeling look resting permanently in the dark gray depths of those eyes.

Shortly after noon, Shelby's vigil was rewarded. Braden and Major Ormsby rode at the head of the scruffiest bunch of men Shelby had ever seen. Most of them, almost too drunk to stay atop their mounts, brandished assorted weapons obviously gathered in haste from every household in the towns and camps at the foot of the Sierras.

She alerted Sam and he hurried out to greet the leaders

of the motley group of soldiers. Though anxious to see Braden, Shelby was apprehensive. Would he be glad to see her again, or weary of his decision to father an orphan "kid"? Perhaps, in these intervening weeks, he had already abandoned the idea, and her as well.

Shelby remained in the corral, keeping herself as inconspicuous and as far from the agitated mob as possible. She would give Braden time to seek her out, if he wanted to. If not, she would know he hadn't missed her, didn't care for her, probably considered her a nuisance he was glad to relinquish to Sam.

Braden dismounted, and leaving Major Ormsby to fill Sam and the others in on the details of the destruction of the stations to the west, led his horse directly to the corral.

Suddenly shy, Shelby hung back against the tack-room door. Braden stood t the gate looking over the milling animals until he spotted her. A smile of recognition began the way she remembered it—slow and steady, creasing the deep furrows along his mouth. But this time the smile spread to his eyes, dispersing the hard expression that usually clouded them.

"What's the matter, kid?" he called and opened the gate. "Not scared of six thousand furious Indians, are you?"

Her heart leaped at his obvious joy in finding her, and Shelby returned his smile as she sprinted over to help him with the gate. "Not as scared as I am of the drunken men goin' out to fight 'em."

Braden scanned the ragged ranks, now beginning to dismount and stagger about, cursing the Indians and shouting threats of retaliation at the sky.

"A mighty sorry-looking bunch, I'll admit. Figure they're going to ride out, shoot up the Indian camp at Pyramid Lake, capture the best-looking women, and ride victorious back to Carson City." He shook his head. "I can't understand why Bill Ormsby let himself be talked into leading such a campaign. He knows Chief Numaga and the Paiutes better than that."

Shelby took Braden's horse. "You goin' out with 'em

to hunt Indians?" she asked as she flipped the stirrup over the saddle horn and prepared to unsaddle the sturdy sorrel mustang.

"Haven't decided. I'm not real eager to be around when they start shooting. Have a feeling their aim may not be too good." Braden gestured toward the swirling mob and tipped his hat to the back of his head.

Shelby tied the horse to a corral post. "Mr. Russell, I need to talk to you."

"Sounds serious," he said, giving her a sharp look.

"It is." While she unfastened the saddle and slipped the bridle off, Shelby told him the details of the Williams' Station burning.

"So that's the way of it. Makes a lot more sense than anything I've heard so far. I'm only sorry I wasn't there to see those thieving sons of perdition get what they deserved."

"Can't you tell Major Ormsby what really happened and stop this war before it gets any worse?" she begged.

They turned to look at the undisciplined mob swarming over the wagon yard. Braden shook his head. "Don't guess they'd listen. They want to go out and be heroes, and nothing you or I could say would change things now. This has been building for three days and nights."

Angered by Braden's seeming indifference, Shelby stamped her foot. "But, sir, we have to try!"

He merely shook his head and walked into the saloon through the tack room.

Shelby slammed the saddle onto the fence and hooked the bridle over the saddle horn. Men! They never seemed to understand the important things. Too angry with Braden to go inside just yet, she pretended to busy herself with a lame horse.

The army poured in and out of Sam's, and Shelby repeatedly heard the expanded versions of the burning of Williams' Station. She finally understood what Braden had been trying to tell her. Painful as it was to admit, she knew now that no amount of talking could dissuade the group from their determination to teach those heathen savages a lesson. It didn't matter that the Indians were well-disciplined, well-armed, and well-mounted, while the would-be conquering heroes were intoxicated, irrational, virtually unarmed and would ride anything with four legs. Major Ormsby was undoubtedly a capable leader, but his troops were undisciplined and drunk. The mission didn't stand the chance of an icicle in August.

Shelby sighed hopelessly and prayed that Braden had sense enough not to join the fight.

Brawling soon broke out among the men, and Major Ormsby and Braden were called out to set things straight. The major called Braden aside, and Shelby watched their intense conversation. Braden nodded occasionally, then gave the major a quick salute as he hurried toward the corral.

"Get my horse," he ordered Shelby. "We're moving on to Williams' Station."

Shelby wanted to yell at him, plead with him, sob her love for him, but instead, she grabbed a rope hanging on a nearby fence post and expertly flipped the loop over the pony's head.

"Getting right smart with that lasso, aren't you?" Braden commented.

"I should be. I happen to do this for a living."

Shelby surprised even herself by the calm manner in which she hauled the pony to the fence and tied him. None of her inner turmoil seemed visible.

Not taking kindly to the termination of his freedom, the pony refused to cooperate when Shelby tried to put the bit between his teeth. Grateful for the distraction, she gave herself over fully to it, pushing Braden's imminent departure and the frightening consequences into the back of her mind.

*You miserable hunk of horseflesh!* Shelby raged silently. *Don't you dare balk on me when I'm trying to impress Braden with my expertise.* She shoved her thumb behind its back teeth. Surprised, the horse opened his mouth and Shelby stuffed the bit inside. She quickly slipped the animal's ears through the bridle and buckled the straps together at the base of his neck.

At last she could fake her lack of concern no longer

and found voice enough to say, "You said you might not go with the army to fight the Indians."

"Don't think I will. But I hate to leave Bill to manage this bunch alone. Most of them have never been out this far from Carson City. If I can help him get them bedded tonight at Williams's and off in the right direction in the morning, I think I ought to."

"But you're helpin' send 'em to certain death."

Braden bristled. "You don't know that."

"I do!" The frustration of not being treated as an adult was rubbing raw. "I saw those Indians. They didn't fool around. They were dignified and sure of themselves." She looked out over the unruly mob. "Not like these men. And you told me yourself that Chief Numaga was wise and disciplined . . . and he's had three days to plan his defense!"

Shelby felt an unreasoning hysteria rise within. Braden wasn't giving her words any more consideration than had Sam. She bought time to bring her emotions under control by concentrating on pinning the shying horse against the corral fence. Stroking his neck and crooning to him, she calmed the wiry little beast before hoisting the heavy saddle to his back.

All the while her mind raced. What could she say that would change things? She would never forgive herself if she didn't do all she could to stop these poor blind wretches from riding into the jaws of death.

Shelby tried again, her façade slipping in her desire to convince Braden that he must stop this foolish attack. "The Indians are defending their homes and families. They have a lot more at stake than these men out for revenge against imagined insults."

Braden took the reins she handed him. "Don't underestimate hatred. Many of these men have had wives and children killed or hurt by Indians elsewhere. This is the first time there have been reinforcements to take on any kind of retaliation."

"But the Paiutes weren't responsible for what happened to their families."

"True. But, to most of them, an Indian is an Indian.

Get even with one, you've paid for damages done by others."

"That's silly. It was some Indians killed my pa, but it was also white men. I don't want to hurt these people. I want justice done to the ones who did the act."

A hard-muscled arm slid around her shoulders. "But Shelby, fifteen-going-on-thirty, few people have your wisdom at any age."

She looked up into his glistening eyes. For a brief moment, his eyes reflected a deep inner emotion. Then, just as quickly, they shuttered and she was staring again into unfeeling granite.

"You stay inside and if there should be an attack here before I get back, hide in the tack room behind the grain sacks. I'll look for you there. Don't try to run unless they set the place afire." Braden gave her shoulder a squeeze and swung quickly into the saddle.

With a sigh of resignation, Shelby opened the gate for him. It would be hopeless to try to persuade him further.

She watched him ride into the midst of the milling troops, shouting instructions as he went. The army formed ragged columns, and with Major Ormsby and Braden at their head, proceeded east.

Someone raised a rusty scarred shotgun. "An Indian for breakfast and a pony to ride!" he cried as he passed the corral.

Shelby, her heart filled with anguish, looked into his hate-filled eyes and wondered if the man would even be alive by breakfast time tomorrow.

## CHAPTER 13

THOSE AT BUCKLAND'S eager for battle left with the straggling army. When the dust cleared, only Shelby, Sam, and the pony rider, Billy Richardson, remained.

"Them guys is crazy. Indians'll eat *them* for breakfast," Billy said. "I seen too many remains after the braves got through. I got no desire to ride near 'em." Nervously he paced the wagon yard, watching the column of dust in the east growing smaller and smaller.

Shelby knew Billy was right in his assessment of the army, and she, too, carried memories of what Indians could do. Thinking of Braden perhaps going to his death, she paced beside Billy while he told of the scalpings and mutilations he had witnessed as a young boy. The more he talked, the more frightened he became, and the more uneasy he made her.

Finally Shelby could stand it no longer. "Billy, stop it! What good is that kind of talk? You're scarin' the livin' daylights out of all of us—yourself, too! How're you gonna ride on east when Bartoles gets here with the mochila?"

Billy turned tortured eyes to her. "I think I'm gonna be sick," he said, whirling about.

Sam opened the door in time to see Billy, on a dead

run, disappear around the corner of the station. "What's the matter with him?"

"I think he's got the liver scared out of him, thinkin' about ridin' out into Indian country with them on the warpath."

"Well, he'd better get over his problem soon. J.B.'s due any time now." Sam's voice held no sympathy for the terrified young man. "And why're you standin' around? Get that pony saddled!" Sam spun on his heel and slammed the door behind him.

Slowly Shelby recoiled the rope she had used to snag Braden's pony, carefully eyeing the stock as she did so. Choosing the right horse for the ride tonight could make the difference in Billy's getting the mail through safely. He would need one that was well-rested and with plenty of stamina in case he had to outrun the fast Indian ponies.

She spotted a chestnut for which she had a special attachment. He was nearly wild, but he could run like greased lightning, or so J. B. Bartoles said. Edging around the corral, she let the rope fly.

She always prepared for battle when she wanted this particular horse, and he didn't disappoint her tonight. Before she had gotten him snubbed tight against a fence post, he had dragged her around the corral several times and, rearing to his hind legs, threatened to stomp her into the ground. She leaned against the corral fence winded, bruised, and dripping with sweat.

"I swear I'd put a bullet in you," Shelby gasped, "if you weren't such a good horse. You're the orneriest critter God ever put on the face of this earth!"

Succeeding at last in saddling the pony, Shelby went inside for some supper. She hadn't eaten since breakfast and she was starved. Absentmindedly, Sam dished her some stew, and Shelby followed his glance to the ticking mantel clock. Nearly six o'clock. J.B. was late, almost an hour late.

"Billy eaten?" she asked.

Sam shook his head. "Says he's sick."

Shelby looked at the small form stretched out on the

cot by the fireplace. His face was turned toward the wall, but Shelby could see from her position across the room that his body was wracked with chills. He was obviously not well. Not well at all.

A ghastly premonition stabbed through her. "Who's goin' to take the mail?" she asked Sam.

Sam's eyes narrowed and turned hard. "He is, if I have to throw 'im on that horse and tie 'im to the horn."

Shelby ate her stew, keeping a wary eye on Billy. His condition seemed to be getting steadily worse. His trips outside grew more frequent until he was so weak he could barely stand. Shelby, all the while praying for his instant recovery, placed a large tin can next to his bed so he could throw up without leaving the comfort of the cabin.

She touched his forehead. It radiated an unhealthy heat. "He's awfully sick," she said to Sam, who refused to come near Billy.

"He's a yellow-striped coward, that's what he is!" Sam raged. "He was fit until it came near time for him to ride. And you can bet your next month's pay, he'll be cured when the mail's gone on east without 'im."

Panic seized Shelby. *Oh, dear God. Is Sam planning for me to take the mail? I don't know the country even that well by daylight. By night, I'd get lost for sure!*

Shelby cleared her throat and tried to swallow over a tongue suddenly gone dry. "You expectin' me to make the ride?" she asked in a croaking whisper.

Sam gave a harsh laugh. "Not unless you're the last resort. You ain't scarcely dry behind the ears. I sure don't intend puttin' a man's job on a boy's shoulders." He gave her a searching look. "'Specially when they're as puny as yours."

Distant hoofbeats brought Sam and Shelby to their feet. Sam grabbed the lantern and dashed out the door. Shelby followed and rushed to the corral for the horse. The pace of the arriving rider was much slower than usual.

"I don't like the sound of that," Sam muttered. "Get my gun."

Shelby raced inside and came back with Sam's repeating rifle.

He handed her the lantern, and taking the gun, flipped the bullet into the chamber. Ready, they stood waiting as the hooves echoed on the bridge. A jaded horse and spent rider crossed the Carson and came into the circle of light cast by the lantern.

"Bob Haslam! What in tarnation you doin' here?" Sam asked, surprise filling his face and voice.

Bob slid off the horse and handed the mochila to Shelby, who placed it over the wooden saddle frame on the relief pony. Sam, in turn, unlocked the way box and marked Bob's time of arrival.

"Come inside, boy, and have some food. You look plumb tuckered." Sam held the door for the weary rider.

Bob collapsed into a chair, and Shelby set a bowl of hot stew and a cup of coffee in front of him. Sam speared some slices of fresh sourdough bread from a loaf Shelby had cut and offered it to him, then sat across from him as Bob attacked the stew.

At last, having eaten his fill, Bob told the story of whites conscripting all the horses in Carson City for the hastily organized army and Indians burning out swing stations, killing the attendants, and driving off the change horses. "I had no choice but to keep comin'."

"I thought J. B. Bartoles was ridin' this leg," Sam said, leaning over the table in tense interest.

"He was, until he ran into that mess at Williams's. He asked me to trade routes with 'im. Don't matter to me where, so long as I get to ride."

With his fingernail, Sam traced a deep scar on the table top. At last, clearing his throat, but keeping his eyes downcast, he asked, "Don't suppose you'd feel up to takin' the mail on east?" He nodded in Billy Richardson's direction. "He's took sick and growed too weak to sit a horse."

Bob turned to regard the shivering man huddled under a stack of quilts.

The silence in the room grew heavier and heavier until Shelby thought she would faint with the waiting. She knew that if Bob didn't soon agree, Sam would ask her to take the run. But he had already ridden seventy-five miles that day. Surely it was too much to ask of a man.

Suddenly Sam shoved his chair back and stood. Resting his hands on the table, he leaned over Bob. "Would you be willin' to make the ride for an extra fifty dollars?"

Shelby couldn't believe her ears. That was as much as the riders made in a month, and Sam was offering it for one ride!

Bob twiddled a spoon in his fingers and stared at the bowl as it caught the lantern rays, giving off glints of light. "Sure. Why not?" he said after a lengthy silence.

Then he, too, rose, and with slightly unsteady steps, walked over and picked up Sam's repeating Spencer rifle. "I'd better take this. Is it loaded?"

Sam gave an audible sigh of relief. "Yep. Even got a bullet in the chamber."

Bob Haslam adjusted the Colt revolver on his hip and jammed an extra loaded cylinder in his pocket. Cradling the Spencer over the crook of his arm, he nodded to Shelby. "Got a pony for me?"

"Ready and waiting." Shelby, not wanting to give Bob time to change his mind, dashed outside and brought the horse to the front door.

He leaped into the saddle, shoved the rifle into the holster at the front, and without a backward glance, spurred the eager mustang into a full gallop. Shelby watched until the trail of dust was no longer visible in the moonlight.

*Keep him safe, Lord,* she prayed. *And watch over Braden. Give him the words and the power to stop this war that's about to start. But if that's not possible, please don't let him get caught up in the hysteria and decide to fight the Indians.*

She waited awhile longer before turning in. In the distance a coyote howled, moaning and yapping in its lost lonely way. Another answered from upriver, telling of men and horses invading their hunting grounds. Shelby knew that by dawn a pack of them would creep through the sagebrush and up to the corral, making the stock restless. This always woke her and she would lie waiting for them to slink away before the horses settled down again.

Just as she started back inside, a pony nickered and stamped the ground as the first coyote yowled closer. The sound sent shivers up Shelby's spine. Maybe it wasn't a coyote, she thought. Maybe it was an Indian signal. She raced inside the station and bolted the heavy door. Still breathing hard, she ignored Sam standing at the window and threw herself on her bed.

She turned her face to the wall and clamped the pillow over her head to drown out the howling. Much later, she felt a hand on her shoulder. Rolling over, she looked into Sam's intense eyes.

"Better keep a pistol handy tonight," he said and handed her the Colt .44, the one Papa had. "You do know how to shoot it, don't you?" he asked.

While Sam watched, Shelby broke out the cylinder to see if it was loaded. Her hands were sure and steady as she snapped the cylinder back into place and hefted the gun for balance. Satisfied with the weapon, she tucked it under her pillow and looked at him with innocent eyes. "I might be able to get off a bullet without shooting myself in the foot," she said.

"Humph," was his only reply as he stalked away to his bed behind the bar.


The men were finally bedded and the camp quiet. Braden hunkered down by a small fire, the restlessness inside him making sleep impossible. He'd had that feeling ever since leaving Shelby at Buckland's this afternoon. Braden had worried for days that the kid wouldn't be there or would have shifted his loyalties to Sam. But Shelby had seemed real glad to see him, and Braden was embarrassed to admit, even to himself, how relieved and delighted he had been when he spotted the little runt crouched in the doorway to the tack room.

Not wanting to face the decision he knew he soon must make—whether to fight his friend Numaga or go back for

136

Shelby and head east away from this growing madness—Braden picked up a willow and absentmindedly poked at the hot coals. In the quietness he fell to remembering the past when things were good—memories that always soothed him and had been a part of him before Shelby.

He leaned back against his saddle and saw the high mountain ranch where he had lived with his father and sister. He saw the two-story log house he had helped build with his own hands, the horses and cattle peacefully grazing in rich pastureland. He saw Jane Ann as she worked beside him, sat at supper with him, made a good life with Pa.

On the nights which numbered over a hundred now, when he camped in aching solitude by lonely fires, he relived their days together. In memory he followed his sister through her day's simple duties, rode with her over their acres, shared in driving their beef to the gold and silver mines in California and Nevada, and took the profits to increase the herds.

Always, he had looked for a woman to be his wife, but none could compete with Jane Ann. After a while, he stopped looking.

He tried to concentrate on her beautiful, slow smile and low, husky voice. Strange how like Jane Ann's voice was Shelby Jackson's. When the kid talked, it drove Braden's grief deeper and deeper and fired his determination to continue the search for Jane Ann's killers.

But tonight the memories wouldn't come right. Instead of thinking of his sister, he found himself dwelling on the short visit with Shelby. The kid's big eyes, begging him not to go with the army in the morning, pleading with him to come back to Buckland's, haunted Braden.

Braden even thought about praying, but it had been so long he wasn't sure God was listening. Besides, he'd never been the kind to beg for anything, and he couldn't see the virtue in starting now.

Stretching out, he stared into the sky. The stars hung low and bright and the Dipper told him it was about two hours past midnight. He felt awake and impatient. Though he still hadn't fully decided if he would join in the attack on the Paiutes, the fever of action burned hot. Finally, he lost consciousness, his mind still in a turmoil.

Shelby couldn't get comfortable. She tossed on the little cot while Braden slipped into her mind even more easily than usual tonight. When at last she slept, her thoughts turned into dreams, ugly vicious dreams which brought her upright, dripping with sweat.

Outside, she could hear the telltale sounds of coyotes nearby, and she got up, glad for any action which might banish her troubled thoughts. Not dwelling long on the notion that the sounds could be Indians rather than coyotes, she crawled out of the warm bed, slipped the bolt, and hurried into the wagon yard to chase the animals away.

Upon her return, she closed the door as quietly as squeaking hinges would allow and tiptoed across the dirt floor.

"Who's up?" came a whispered question from the direction of the bar.

Sam's voice, unexpected at this hour, startled Shelby. She lost her bearings and kicked a chair. "Sam? What are you doin' awake?"

"That's no kinda answer. You sick, too?" He sounded genuinely concerned.

"No. Just out sendin' the coyotes home. Don't like my horses spooked."

"*Your horses?* Funny, I thought they belonged to the Pony," Sam growled and came from behind the bar to throw more logs on the fire.

Though the words were sharp, the tone of his voice said he wanted to talk. The moon had set and it was nearly daylight before Sam stopped his reminiscing and Shelby slid wearily under the covers.

A sound like distant thunder woke her. Sunlight streamed across the floor, and someone was pounding on the door hard enough to take it off the hinges. On his way to the door, Sam raked thin fingers through tousled hair at the same time he tried to pull up his suspenders.

"All right! All right! Keep yer shirt on!" he hollered as he fumbled with the heavy bolt.

But the determined pounding went on.

"What's going on in there?" came a voice from outside.

Braden! *Oh, thank you Lord*, Shelby prayed fervently. He had decided not to fight after all and had come back for her.

## CHAPTER 14

ONE DAY AFTER THE ATTACK on Chief Numaga's Paiutes on the eleventh of May, distant columns of smoke could be seen in any direction one cared to look.

There had been no news of Bob Haslam or the ragtag army, and Braden paced the floor. He wore a look black enough to frighten even the most daring of his friends, and Shelby, not counted in that group, kept out of his way by washing the glasses and cleaning the shelves behind the bar.

Sam, turning from the window, reported, "Don't look real good out there. I'd guess the Indians won and they're burnin' and killin' everything in their path."

From his bed Billy Richardson reached out, and for the hundredth time, checked the cylinder of the seven-bullet repeater rifle resting against the wall near his head. Watching Billy set the gun back in its place, Shelby's hand brushed the holster attached to her hip.

Braden joined Sam at the window. They stood without speaking, but the slump of their shoulders made it plain they were worried.

Sam suddenly whirled about and stalked behind the bar. With trembling hands he poured himself a glass of whiskey. "Can't hardly stand to think of Bob out there tryin' to get the mail through," he said before tossing down the liquor.

Braden's knuckles whitened as he gripped the window sill. "You don't need to excuse getting yourself drunk, Sam. Admit you're scared witless, kill the bottle, and get crocked. Then, when we need your gun, you'll be passed out in the corner." He sent a piercing look through the frightened man. "With a sick man armed with a rifle and a runt of a kid shooting a revolver, we won't miss you much. Three of us can hold off the Paiute nation, no trouble at all."

Shamefaced, Sam set the bottle back under the bar, and he and Braden resumed their pacing.

Eventually Sam paused in front of the fireplace and stretched out his hands to warm them. "Cain't remember a colder May," he said distractedly, as if making idle conversation would return life to normalcy.

Shelby responded by throwing another log on the still-glowing embers. "I'll go fetch some more wood," she said in an off-handed manner and started to unbolt the door.

Sam dashed across the room and cut her off. "You go near that door," he said in a low growl, "and I'll blow a hole in you."

Astonished, Shelby froze. A revolver quivered in his hand, and a frightening madness glittered from his penetrating eyes. She gulped and sent a frantic look toward Braden.

Silently he stepped behind Sam and poked his gun into the distraught man's back. "Let me have your gun. You're too scared to know who's the enemy. You wouldn't want to shoot a friend, now would you?"

Sam's face knotted into hate-filled lines and he whipped around. "You touch me and you're a dead man!" he snarled at Braden.

Braden knocked the gun from Sam's hand and sent it spinning across the floor. Shelby leaped for the revolver and shoved it along to Billy. He reached out and grabbed it.

"I think you'd better take a nap," Braden said, and

gripping Sam's arm, shoved him toward his cot behind the bar. Meekly Sam submitted, and under the effects of the drink on an empty stomach, was soon snoring.

"Do you suppose it's safe enough to get some wood?" Shelby asked.

"Not safe *enough*, but go on. We can't stay penned up like chickens," Braden said, throwing back the bolt. "I'll keep you covered, but don't take all day."

Shelby eased out into the fresh air of late afternoon. The woodpile was only a short distance away, but it seemed like miles. She looked carefully in all directions before venturing toward it.

She quickly filled the crook of her arm with split logs and hurried back toward the station. Hearing something from the east, however, she stopped to listen.

"What's the matter?" Braden called.

"I think the Pony's coming."

"Hurry up and get in here!" he shouted.

Shelby dashed through the door and dumped her load in the empty corner woodbox. "I need to saddle a horse," she said, starting back outside.

A grip of iron hauled her to an abrupt stop. "You don't know for sure it's the Pony. Maybe you should stay put until you do." Braden slammed and bolted the door. "Billy, get your carcass off that bed and set your rifle at the front window. I'll take the back one. Sam!" he shouted at the man, who raised a tousled head from his pillow. "Get your gun and hide behind the door. If they try to break in, shoot and ask questions later. Shelby, stay down behind the bar but keep your gun handy."

For the next few moments Shelby's heart was in her throat. She couldn't face the idea that a host of war-maddened Indians might be attacking this pitiful little spot and instead, turned her thoughts to a spring day last year in Missouri, when she had hoed weeds in her little garden.

"I think I hear only one horse," Billy pointed out. "Doubt one Indian would come by hisself to do damage."

Shelby didn't wait for permission but raced through

142

the tack room and out into the corral to prepare a pony. In the distance a rise of dust signaled the rider's progress. Though her hands trembled, Shelby soon had a mustang roped and saddled. Braden and Sam, still holding their rifles, waited in the wagon yard as drumming hoofbeats drew closer.

Shelby climbed the corral fence until she could lean over the top rail. With the added height she was the first to recognize the rider. "It's Bob Haslam!" she called.

"That's not news," Sam said in a sour voice. "He's supposed to be the one bringin' the mail. Too bad he's alone. Hoped he'd find someone with a spine to take Richardson's place."

"That's enough, Sam," Braden snapped and turned his back. "How goes it?" he asked as the pony slid to a stop and Bob sprang out of the saddle, mochila in hand.

Shelby grabbed the reins and began walking the winded animal. She stayed close enough, however, to hear Bob's story.

"Going east, never sighted a Paiute in the whole hundred miles to Smith Creek," Bob said as he fitted the mochila over the saddle of the fresh pony. "Picked up new mounts on schedule at Sink of the Carson, Sand Springs, and Cold Springs."

"About the same on your return trip?" Braden asked.

Though the question was voiced casually enough, Shelby knew how desperately Braden waited word.

Bob looked uneasy. "I found the station master at Cold Springs dead and the horses scattered."

The muscles in Braden's jaw clenched, his only acknowledgment of the grim news.

"What did you do?" Shelby gasped.

"There wasn't no turnin' back, so I watered my horse, who was pretty tired after ridin' thirty miles. Sand Springs was thirty miles on down the road, but I started anyway."

"Weren't you scared?" Shelby asked.

Bob answered that with a disdainful look. "When I rode into Sand Springs, there was only one man to tend the place. When I told him what I'd found at Cold

Springs, it didn't take much persuasion for him to saddle up and make the run with me to the Sink of the Carson. The men there were well barricaded. They had sighted war parties, and with the news of Ormsby's defeat, the tenders was expectin' an attack any time. The man from Cold Springs stayed to help, but I whipped up a fresh horse and here I am."

Braden looked stunned. "Ormsby's defeat?"

"I guess it was pretty awful. Some of the survivors found their way into the station at the Sink. Said there was Indians waitin' for 'em at the Truckee River. Ormsby's men never had a chance. Numaga fought a real smart battle. After Ormsby was killed, that ended any hope the army had. Men holdin' the retreat route weren't there, and the Paiutes cut what was left of the army to pieces."

Braden swore under his breath and stomped off. His departing footsteps sent out a harsh echo from the wooden planks of the bridge.

Shelby's heart ached for Braden. He was probably blaming himself for the death of his friend. After giving him a parting glance, she led the overheated horse around the side of the station out of the wind. As she continued walking him, she pondered Braden's dilemma. With his heavy burden of grief and guilt over his family, this new loss might be too much to bear. *Please, God, help Braden understand he had nothing to do with Major Ormsby's defeat. Don't let him feel a need to avenge this death, too.*

While Sam unlocked the way box, Bob walked over to the bucket for a cup of water.

"Come on inside and rest fer a spell," Sam urged. "I'll fix you some grub."

"Can't. Mail was nine hours late comin' into Smith Creek. Gave me a rest after that hundred and seventy-five mile ride from Friday's Station, but I'm already late gettin' it on west."

Bob sprang into the saddle and was off again. Shelby watched until the dust from his pony grew faint, and she was reminded to ask the Lord to protect him, too. *What an incredible ride the man has made,* she thought. *He will have ridden over three hundred and eighty miles of death and desert in two days by the time he gets back to Friday's Station.* The hundred-dollar bonus he would receive suddenly seemed pitifully inadequate.

When she awakened the next morning, Shelby found Braden, his face haggard from lack of sleep, staring into the small fire and poking at the glowing coals with a stick.

"Mr. Russell?" she ventured.

He turned bloodshot eyes on her—eyes filled with the agony of his grief.

Shelby bit her lip. She longed to take him in her arms, but in her present role, she was helpless to comfort him. Unable to bear the intensity of Braden's pain, she studied the pile of logs at length before selecting a small one and carefully placing it on the faltering fire. She again looked at the suffering man. He remained in unapproachable misery, shutting out those around him.

Drawing a heart in the dirt floor with her toe, Shelby wondered what she should be doing. Sam stared morosely out the window at the desert to the west, and Billy's bed was empty.

Upon closer inspection, Shelby noticed his gun and personal belongings were gone. *He surely hasn't ridden out into the fury Bob reported yesterday.* Shelby hurried into the tack room and took a quick inventory of the equipment. They were short one saddle. Billy had gone.

Shelby ran into the corral. He had chosen one of the better horses. She wondered which direction he had decided to ride. From the numerous thin trails of smoke spiraling upward against the horizon at every turn, it didn't look safe anywhere. As she watched, small dots appeared on the horizon to the northwest.

Shelby ran back to the tack room for the field glasses. Under magnification, she could see a cluster of slump-shouldered men slogging toward the station, their feet raising small puffs of white dust as they dragged along. They had to be survivors from the defeated army that

145

had set off with such confidence only day before yesterday.

"Sam!" she hollered into the silent saloon. "Soldiers comin'. What do you want me to do?"

Sam came alive and began barking orders. Shelby flew to set tables and slice bacon while Sam started mixing biscuit dough. Braden left his spot by the fire and raced out the door. This was his chance for firsthand news of William Ormsby.

It seemed hours before the wounded were treated and all the stragglers cleaned and fed, but at last Shelby was free to curl up in a corner and give her full attention to the talk swirling about her. Tales of heroism and cowardice, incomprehensible brutality and life-preserving gentleness mingled to give a contradictory picture of the fight.

"One man I'd like to get my hands on," began a wrinkled old-timer near Shelby, "is that yellow-bellied quitter what left the pass unprotected when we was ordered to retreat. Never forget that traitorous skunk long as I live."

"What'd he look like?" asked another. "I'll keep a lookout for him, too. He's the reason we got cut up so bad."

"There were two of 'em, but he was the biggest braggart I ever heard—and I've heard some in my day—a flabby feller with hanging jowls and big, hammy hands."

Elwood P. Hawker! Shelby heard no more. What was he doing with the army? He hadn't appeared the type to become involved in any unpleasantness unless there was a profit to be made. Perhaps he had merchandise to sell to the volunteers and took off after he had made money off their misfortune. That would fit her impressions of him.

"Shelby!"

Braden's voice thundered above her. She raised startled eyes to his.

"Get a couple of horses saddled. We're riding into

Carson City. That's going to be the safest place for you until this thing blows over."

Without waiting for her reaction, he gathered his bedroll and swung through the tack room door for his saddle. Shelby leaped to her feet and hurriedly followed his example.

With Braden to help, they were soon mounted and riding west.

After a while, Shelby ventured a question. "Why do you suppose Elwood P. Hawker was with the army? He didn't seem the sort to put himself out for any causes that didn't put money in his pocket."

"Also placed himself where he could escape if the battle didn't go well. Because of him and his friend, a lot of men were killed." Braden's tone was bitter.

"Do you suppose the men who traveled with us and stayed to work at Roberts' Station are still there?"

"I don't know, but I intend to find out. Hiring them has always bothered me."

Though little conversation passed between them after that, Shelby noticed that the set of Braden's shoulders gradually relaxed, and his face assumed a more pleasant countenance. It was hard for anyone to be angry on such a beautiful day, Shelby thought with satisfaction.

May was winning the battle with the savage winter. Though it was still cold at night, by midday the sun had warmed the air to a comfortable temperature, the first Shelby had experienced in her five-month stay in the desert.

Late that evening they rode into Carson City. The hysterical town bristled with fortifications. Word had been sent to California for men and supplies to ward off what all believed to be an imminent Indian attack. Now troops were headquartered here and kept a wary eye on the smoke signals in the desert to the northeast.

Ormsby House was transformed. The once festive atmosphere was now charged with grief and despair.

"Braden!" Elizabeth exclaimed as they entered the lobby. "I've prayed you would come. I don't think I could bear this without you."

Braden cradled the grieving woman in his arms, and she clung to him, seeming to draw strength from his presence.

Shelby, embarrassed to be witnessing the tender scene, mumbled an excuse for leaving and vanished outside. She didn't return to Ormsby House until dark.

While making her way through the lobby, the desk clerk directed her to a closet of a room where Shelby found her things piled in the middle of a small cot. She didn't mind. She would be spared the frustration of sharing a room with Braden. Besides, this was the first privacy she had enjoyed for months. Cramped as it was, this solitary space was a luxury, and she gave thanks for it.

And there was time to think, to collect her wits. With the world turned upside down, Shelby was jobless, her only money being the pay she had received for one month's work for the Pony. Thirty dollars wouldn't take care of her for long. She was going to have to find other employment immediately.

Shelby stretched out on the bed to ponder her situation, but the long day caught up with her, and she suddenly realized Braden was shaking her.

"Come on, kid. Get out of the quilts. It's time we rode."

Rubbing the sleep from her eyes, she asked, "Where to?"

"From all I can gather, the Paiutes are spending their anger on the folks here at the foot of the mountains. Seems to me farther east will be safer. Those two eastern tinhorns left the Pony high and dry soon as the going got rough. They need tenders at Roberts' Station and Egan Canyon Station. Egan's only a swing station, but Bolivar wants you there for now."

While he talked Shelby pulled on her boots and ran a dirty palm over her hair before taming it under the slouch hat. "Suppose I could wash and eat before we go?"

"Wash?" Braden looked at her in amazement.

Shelby gulped at her slip. "I do, on occasion," she said gruffly in an attempt to cover up.

"Don't dawdle. We need supplies and a pack mule. Can't count on stations along the way to house us this trip. Safest to travel at night when the Indians aren't as eager, so I want to be ready to start about sunset. Soon as you eat, bring up a mule from the Pony corral while I start gathering the essentials at the store."

Shelby dashed cold water over her face and hands before gulping down a bowl of mush. Then, she dashed out of the hotel, rounded the corner on her way to the Pony office, and almost ran headlong into a large man hurrying along the street. Without looking at her, he brushed her out of his way with a huge, beefy hand and continued swiftly on his way.

Shelby, however, recognized the hand and the man. Elwood P. Hawker! What was he doing here in Carson City, where he was scarcely welcome?

## CHAPTER 15

THE WIND BLEW STEADILY from the northwest that last Tuesday in October. Wispy cloud tails darkened as they gathered over the desert far to the east of Buckland's

Shelby worried her way through the day, wore it out starting little jobs, never finishing any of them. She sensed eyes on her as though Egan Canyon Station were being watched, and time and again she stopped to scan the high mountain meadow, dressed in bedraggled autumn foliage.

After each fruitless search Shelby forced herself to return to her tasks, but an unexplainable restlessness stirred through her, at times making her ornery as a mule with a burr under the pack frame. At other times, she shivered with anticipation of a thing she couldn't quite grasp. By nightfall, she was exhausted from the strain and relieved when Aunt Ruby, the station tender's wife, called her for supper.

After the three of them were assembled and prayers said, Aunt Ruby commented, "I've had the strangest feeling today. Like someone has been watching nearly every move we've made. You notice anything out of the ordinary, Pete?"

Her husband nodded. "Thought it was just me. Comfortin' to know it wasn't."

"Kinda felt the same way," Shelby confessed.

Aunt Ruby gave a relieved sigh and plumped onto her chair. "Well then, guess there's no cause to doubt my sanity, after all. Folks in Salt Lake City warned us about bein' station tenders for the Pony so far from civilization. Was beginnin' to think they were right."

Nerves always affected Shelby's stomach and tonight she wasn't very hungry.

Aunt Ruby noticed. "Got you so upset you're not eatin'," she said. "Shoulda kept my thoughts to myself."

"No. I've felt queer all day. Maybe I've been eatin' too much." Shelby had come to relish the delicious meals since Uncle Pete and Aunt Ruby arrived to take over the station. "Those were fine dumplin's you made last night, and I reckon I made a pig of myself."

"Don't think it's anything you ate," Pete said. "My rheumatics is acting up real bad tonight. I'd bet we're in for our first serious storm."

As if on cue, the wind picked up, howling its determination to end autumn. Strong gusts whistled around the corners of the small stone hut and down the large rock chimney which made up one wall of the small room.

Having finished eating, Pete hobbled across the room to stack more wood on the fire, then returned to his chair at the rude table. A kerosene lantern hanging overhead cast flickering shadows over the table top where Aunt Ruby fingered her red leather Bible in preparation for the evening reading.

Aunt Ruby's coming had turned the barren little cabin into a cozy place, and for the first time since leaving St. Joe, Shelby felt at home. If she could hear more often from Braden, she would be reasonably happy. He had written two letters and visited once since he brought her here last June.

Her greatest desire now was to escape the deception of being a boy and still keep her job with the Pony. She found she liked working with horses and she was good at it, but she wanted Braden Russell to look on her as something far different from a son.

The soft slap as the Book was shut brought Shelby from her reverie. She blinked herself back to the present moment and realized she had heard nothing of the Scripture reading. Nor had she found any solution to the predicament in which she was locked.

The temperature began dropping so rapidly the fire couldn't keep pace, and soon they were shivering.

"Looks like the best place for all of us is in bed," Pete announced. "Leave the dishes for morning, Mother. You look as worn out as I feel."

Aunt Ruby gathered the bowls, stacked them in the dishpan, and poured water over them. "I think you're right. Thank goodness you spent the day restocking our woodpile."

Pete stood and put on his heavy coat. "Shelby, get your horses into the tack room, and we'll open the door between. Their body warmth will help heat our room tonight, and they'll be spared the storm."

Shelby took her coat from its peg above her bed and pulled the cap and mittens from the pockets. Securely bundled against the howling wind, she and Pete hurried to the corral. The horses came willingly into the shelter attached to the cabin, and it took only a few minutes to feed and water the three of them.

All night the wind battered the mountain and by morning had gathered in intensity. Shelby slept little and welcomed daylight as Pete got up to rebuild the fire.

Hearing the stirrings inside the cabin, the horses nickered softly, and with teeth chattering, Shelby pulled on her pants and went to tend them. Giving each horse a friendly pat as she passed by, Shelby gingerly pushed open the door into the corral and looked outside. Though the clock said it was after eight, the sky was layered deep with heavy black clouds. *It was as dismal as the inside of Moses's boot,* Shelby thought, smiling at one of her aunt's favorite sayings.

As she finished tending the animals, snow began lacing the air and shortly a real blizzard raged around the station house. It didn't lessen all day, condemning both men and animals to their cramped quarters.

Pete, a large man, paced out his restive feelings, Aunt Ruby cooked, and Shelby sat at the table practicing chess moves. Braden had casually mentioned playing with Jane Ann, and this was all the incentive Shelby needed to improve her game.

The clock struck two, and Pete paused to look out the single window.

"Sure won't be any records set on the Pony run today," he observed. "In fact, it'll surprise me if Bill Fisher gets through this snowstorm at all." Shuffling over to stand with his back to the fire and warm his hands, he continued, "I've never seen such a blizzard in all my life."

Shelby felt like an old-timer in the face of his pessimism. "You weren't with the Pony when it started. Last spring, Warren Upson crossed the Sierras in a storm when even the oxen from the freight wagons couldn't break the trail. Bill will get through, all right."

But by late afternoon Bill still hadn't arrived, and even Shelby conceded that he might be in trouble.

"Saddle me a horse, Shelby," ordered Pete. "I can't stand it any longer, thinkin' that boy needs help and me sittin' here comfortable in front of a fire."

"You'll stay right here where you belong, Pete," Aunt Ruby declared. "I'm too young to be a widow."

"Besides, it wouldn't do no good," Shelby said from her post at the window. "You couldn't see five feet ahead of you in this storm."

Grim-faced, Pete retreated to his rocker by the fire. "Feel real sorry for anyone has to be out in this. Man or beast'll find the goin' mighty rough."

For the hundredth time, Shelby went to check on the horses in the shelter. She took a shovel and cleaned out their space again before giving them extra hay. When Shelby came back into the cabin, Aunt Ruby had supper on the table. They ate in silence, straining for any sounds of the Pony rider.

By nine o'clock when he still hadn't arrived, Shelby and Pete began pacing in earnest. Aunt Ruby read from the Bible in a quiet voice, but the words gave Shelby no comfort. What if Bill Fisher didn't get through? She shivered as she thought of him riding in the frigid storm up Egan Canyon and extended her perpetually cold hands to the warmth of the bright fire.

At last Aunt Ruby gently closed the Bible. "I'm servin' no good purpose sittin' here worryin'. Think I'll turn in. How about you, Father?"

Pete placed another log on the fire. "I'll keep the watch awhile longer. Sure would hate to be asleep and not help that boy should he call out, needin' me."

With the wind sounding like a freight train at full steam, Shelby wondered how he'd be able to hear anything, but she knew she couldn't sleep either. She stretched out, fully dressed, intending to help Pete keep the vigil.

Hours later, she awoke with a start. Pete still sat in his chair in front of the fireplace, his head sunk low on his chest, rising and falling rhythmically.

Springing to her feet, Shelby cocked her head and listened carefully. There it was again! Above the keening wail of the wind, there was a faint scratching sound.

"Pete!" she shouted, grabbing his shoulder and shaking him awake. "Something's out there!"

The two of them scrambled to reach the door. Shelby arrived first and threw open the slab barricade. There, in the light of early dawn, stood a snow-plastered pony. Shelby started for the nearly frozen animal, tripped over something, and sprawled headlong into the deep snow.

Pete, followed closely behind Shelby and helped roll the snow-encrusted object over. "It's Bill Fisher!" he cried. "Ruby!" he shouted to his wife, but she was already up and standing in the open door.

"Hurry! Get that boy in here and let's see what damage has been done."

Shelby found her footing, and together, she and Pete carried the inert figure inside. They stripped off his outer clothes and stretched him out on Shelby's bed. Aunt Ruby made a quick assessment of his condition.

"His hands and feet are froze. He can't ride out of here."

So exhausted from his ride he could scarcely talk, Bill began to protest.

"Save your breath!" Pete told him. "If the mail never gets no farther than Egan's Station, you ain't goin' nowhere, boy!"

"I'll go," Shelby heard herself volunteering. "He's made a great effort to get it this far. I'm goin' to take it on."

"No, you're not, young man!" Aunt Ruby straightened and fastened Shelby with a withering look.

"I know the route into Ruby Valley. There are two stations between here and there. I won't break any speed records, but I know I can get the mail through."

"Boy's right, Ruby," Pete broke in. "Our job's to see to the mail. Been some important news goin' back and forth about California stayin' with the Union or goin' Confederate. And we got that radical group wants to see the whole Pacific coast secede from both causes and become a separate country." He turned to Shelby. "You're right, boy. Mail needs to go on. Dress yourself in the warmest clothes you own. I'll see to your horse."

While Shelby dressed she listened to the wind drive the snow and slam it against the door. She bit her lip. Was she crazy to go out in this storm? The mail was already so late, what could a few more hours matter? But something told her she had no choice, and she slipped into her knee-high boots.

"Here's some hot tea. Better'n coffee to keep you goin'," Aunt Ruby said, handing Shelby a canteen.

"Which horse you want?" Pete asked as he came in from the tack room.

A stirring in the corner caused Shelby to turn. Bill Fisher, his face gaunt and his eyes hollow, struggled to sit up. "Take the best, most sure-footed animal you got," he croaked. "Need one you can trust—one that trusts you."

Shelby nodded. She knew just the horse. The little gelding had been shot in the Indian uprising, and she had nursed him back to health, giving him a name that described the way his mane curled over his forehead.

"Corkscrew, Pete," she said. "He's the best we got."

"Not that gunshot nag?"

"He'll do fine. We're not runnin' a race. We're only tryin' to get the mail to Ruby Valley and the next rider."

The look on Pete's face said he thought she was crazy, but that was all right. Shelby knew the horse and trusted him. Pete started back into the tack room, then paused. "Kid, I sure hate for you to go out in this blizzard," he said in a low voice. "I'd go myself, but I'm too heavy. Stand a lot better chance of gettin' through with a lighter rider." He took a couple more steps, then turned. "Still, I've a mind not to let you go."

"Storm can't keep up this hard much longer," Shelby pointed out. "Too early in the year. It's nearly mornin' and I know the trail. I'll make it fine."

"You better. Braden Russell'll string me up if anything happens to you."

"And Bolivar Roberts'll string you up if the mail don't go through."

Pete sighed. "Can't win either way."

A few minutes later he was at the front door with Corkscrew saddled and carrying the mochila. Shelby gave Bill a wave and accepted Aunt Ruby's bear hug and Pete's brisk handshake before swinging onto the horse.

"You take care, you hear?" Pete cautioned. "Don't take no chances. Go slow, and if you get so you can't feel your feet, get off and walk a spell."

Shelby looked into the concerned faces of these good people. "Don't worry," she said. "I'll be all right."

"We'll be prayin' for you all the way," Aunt Ruby promised.

Shelby nodded, then turned the pony into the storm. Snow pelted her face, but Corkscrew made good headway down the mountain. Though the wind was sharp at times, it was nothing to worry about. *This trip isn't going to be so hard after all,* she thought as she kept the horse moving at a trot through the pines and rocks. Then Shelby reached an unprotected spot, and the arctic cold of the wind cut through her clothes so that she shivered in spite of her determination not to.

Moving against the battering winds and driving snow, Corkscrew slowed to a walk, and Shelby, slapped in the face with the full force, could scarcely breathe. She ducked her head and grimaced as the chill rapidly destroyed the feeling in her feet and hands. Shelby peered through the blinding snow for some sign of shelter, but the terrain was unfamiliar.

Without warning Corkscrew stopped, refusing to budge another step.

"Come on, boy!" Shelby urged. "We've got to keep moving, or we'll both freeze." She reached out and patted his neck reassuringly.

The little pony snorted, reared his head into the thickening storm, and moved on again. Shelby let the reins drop. It was up to Corkscrew to keep to the trail, for she could see nothing at all.

On they plodded. Ice crystals formed on Shelby's cheeks and lashes, and though she beat on her legs with her fists, she could not recover any feeling below her waist. *Please, dear Lord, help us get through this storm,* she prayed.

Suddenly the horse slipped from the trail and floundered in snow stirrup-deep.

"Take it easy, boy," Shelby crooned as she fought to get him turned around and back on the trail.

But with their tracks obliterated, Shelby couldn't tell which direction to go. Though she urged the horse forward, he bowed his neck and danced sideways. Finally Corkscrew halted and would not respond to any of her commands. What was the matter with him?

Shelby dismounted, gathered the reins, and continued on foot. She had trudged only a few steps when she stumbled against a large fallen log blocking their path. She felt her way around the obstacle, mounted the pony, and they struggled on.

The wind died away, giving the travelers a short respite, then roared back with renewed intensity, lashing them until they both quivered with the unrelenting fury of the storm. Shelby leaned out of the saddle, peering intently through the snow. She brushed against rock and her head dislodged a small avalanche. Startled, the pony shied, nearly unseating Shelby. Stretching out both her hands, she felt rock on either side of her. This was a narrow, unfamiliar canyon, well off the trail to Ruby Valley.

"We're lost, Corkscrew." Saying the words aloud made them more terrifying in their implication, and a paralyzing fear welled inside her and constricted her throat. *Lost! Oh, Lord, where are you?*

The canyon was too narrow for horse and rider to turn around. They had no choice but to go on.

She slapped the pony on the flank. "Let's go, boy. Move along."

Off they went again, bucking the ferocious wind which covered them both with snow. Ice hung from Corkscrew's muzzle, and he shook his head frequently to rid himself of the troublesome substance.

Then the wind changed directions and died down. A hush, broken only by the heavy breathing of the struggling pony, fell over the canyon. Snow continued to fall at a frightening rate, however, and soon Shelby could no longer see even the heaving sides of the small beast beneath her.

She felt the trail descending at a steep angle, and as they broke out of the canyon, the wind howled around them and the cold grew more intense. She hunched into her coat, trying to keep the snow from packing around her collar and sliding under her clothes.

Again Corkscrew halted in his tracks.

"Come on, boy," Shelby urged and gave him an impatient kick in the ribs, but he stood there.

She ranted and railed at him but nothing would move the pony, and after wrenching herself free of the ice imprisoning her in the saddle, Shelby slid off into snow above her hips.

"Corkscrew, I thought you were a good horse, but you're no better than a bullheaded mule!" she scolded. "We'll freeze if we stay here. Now come on!"

Dipping her head against the blinding storm, she gave the reins a tug, then another. Still, the animal remained firmly implanted in his tracks.

Bracing both feet and leaning back, Shelby pulled hard on the reins, determined to move the obstinate creature. Then, with one desperate yank, she felt herself toppling backward—not into softly drifted snow—into nothingness. She was falling, plunging into space, and pulling the bewildered pony down with her.

## CHAPTER 16

BRADEN RODE WITH HIS RIFLE resting across the front of the saddle and his pistol holster unfastened. He felt watching eyes upon him as he traveled along the windswept desert trail to Egan Station. Good. It meant his quarry was being most accommodating, and his long search was nearly over.

Braden had planned this moment for months, ever since his sister's death. This canyon would be a fine place to exact payment in kind for her senseless murder, and in spite of the bitter wind bringing in the first real storm of the season, Braden warmed himself on thoughts of revenge. How sweet it would be to look at last into the faces of the men responsible and watch them cower and beg for life. Hear their pleadings for mercy and denials of any wrongdoing. Smell the fear rise from them as he methodically carried out his plan.

Braden licked the alkali dust from his lips, relishing its biting taste. It matched his mood perfectly. He ran his hand over the butt of the rifle and slipped his index finger over the trigger, feeling the hard metal hook. He tensed the finger and imagined the cowardly face lined up in the sights.

He tried to ignore the lack of feeling inside. There was

no blossoming of joy, no elation as Braden drew nearer the canyon entrance. If anything, he grew more cold and unfeeling the closer he rode to the showdown.

The wind increased in velocity, and laced with snow, it pierced even Braden's warm coat and the muffler wrapped around his throat and face until only his eyes showed. But the storm rapidly worsened until soon he could scarcely see. Only a fool or a Pony Express rider would brave this storm he decided and sought shelter in a shallow cave in the rock wall near the entrance to Egan Canyon.

There was barely room for him and his horse, but the cave, being on the leaward side, offered refuge from the battering wind. Snow drifted across the opening, sealing it, and the body heat radiating from the horse made the haven almost comfortable. It also gave Braden a certain perverse satisfaction to think of his prey suffering, unprotected, in the storm. Made him a mite less anxious to wreak his vengeance immediately.

The night passed, and sometime the next afternoon, the ferocity of the storm abated. Using a branch he found on the floor of the cave, Braden dug through the drift and opened a passage out of his cramped prison.

The sky was still leaden with snow-filled clouds, but he mounted his horse and took advantage of the break in the weather to see his way through Egan Canyon. Now that he knew who he was looking for, Braden could afford to wait. Wanted to wait, let them worry over whether he knew their identity for sure, and if he did, when and where he'd finally confront them. The more antsy they became, the more apt they'd be to make mistakes.

Besides, it had been far too long since he'd visited Shelby. At the thought of seeing the kid, Braden's heart beat in an irregular rush.

Braden let the pony pick a way across the drifted meadow, and he stepped out of the saddle in front of the little cabin. With the horse's hoofbeats muffled by the snow, he wasn't surprised when no one came to greet him. His hand trembled with anticipation as he tied the pony to the corral rail. Why did he feel such a surge of emotion at the thought of Shelby? He couldn't understand it and that bothered him.

Braden, waiting for his knock to be answered, noticed the stock wasn't in the corral and guessed they were being cared for in the tack room. Shelby did a wonderful job with the animals in his care. Kid was a natural when it came to livestock. Best Braden had ever seen.

"Braden!" Pete gasped as he flung open the door.

A shadow flicked over Pete's face, but Braden couldn't translate its meaning and quickly forget about it.

"What craziness brings you out in this storm?" Pete asked and stepped aside to let Braden enter. "Don't stand out there freezin'. Get inside."

Braden stomped off the snow, ducked through the low door and into the cozy room. His eyes fell on a figure stretched out on Shelby's bed, and his heart bounded against his ribs. "Who's that?" he asked, trying to keep the panic under control.

"Bill Fisher. Boy nearly froze to death in last night's storm. More dead than alive when he reached the station," Pete explained.

Braden breathed a sigh of relief. He didn't know what he would do if Shelby should be hurt or get sick. From his reaction just now, he'd likely be more trouble than help.

Ruby left her patient and hurried to greet Braden. "Sit down by the fire, and I'll get you a cup of coffee. Warm you up and hold you over 'til I can get some food on the table."

*Funny Shelby doesn't come in from the tack room to see me*, he thought as he eased out of his coat and hung it on a peg. This wasn't like the kid. He'd always seemed so glad to see Braden on previous visits.

Braden slid into Pete's rocker and accepted the hot cup while Pete filled him in on the story of Bill's ride. Then it hit Braden. *Shelby isn't here. He's taken the mail!*

Trying to maintain his composure, Braden asked in a tight voice, "The kid take the run?"

Pete looked extremely uncomfortable. "He wouldn't

have it no other way." His tone was noticeably defensive. "Insisted the mail had to go through. Might be something important and a delay could make a difference."

Ruby looked up from where she was placing compresses on Bill's frozen feet. "We had no idea the storm would get worse and last so long. Pete and I have worried ourselves sick about the boy, but we don't know what to do."

Braden's insides turned to lead. The thought of that inexperienced little kid out in a killer blizzard made him wild. Only the self-control learned over the past months kept Braden from turning his frustration on Pete and beating him to a pulp. *How could he have let Shelby go? How could he!*

Braden didn't dare speak. And then shock waves rolled through him. Those murdering rascals were out there, too! They'd show the poor little kid no mercy if they found him. Knowing how much Braden cared for Shelby, they'd do something inhumanly cruel to the boy just to get even.

"I need a fresh horse!" Braden shouted as he flew for his coat.

Pete and Ruby froze in their tracks and watched him with fear-widened eyes. Pete, his face white and drawn, tried to speak but only croaks came out.

Braden shot into the tack room and grabbed the halter of the nearest pony. He led it outside, quickly unsaddled his weary pony, and changed the saddle to the fresh horse.

"Here," Ruby called, running through the snow to hand him a package wrapped in oilcloth. "You need to eat and if . . ." There was a self-conscious pause. "When you find Shelby, he'll need food, too."

Shelby plummeted down the face of the cliff, sprawling through space. As she fell, her body twisted and her coat slid up. With no protection save her shirt and undershirt, her middle grazed the sharp rocks protruding through the drifts. And then she felt the impact of flesh on frozen ground, and the bushes and trees, jarred by her hasty descent, released their icy loads and showered her prostrate form with a sprinkling of snow.

She came to momentarily, never realizing she had been unconscious.

"Must have knocked the wind out of me," she mumbled, loath to admit anything worse, for the growing numbness around the base of her chest frightened her.

Shelby rolled over and off the rock into a drift. After sitting up, she shook the snow off her coat and brushed it from her face. She remembered Corkscrew, but when she looked around, she couldn't see the pony. Couldn't hear any sound. The sun was trying to crowd its way through a break in the clouds, and slender rays slanted into the canyon. But there were no familiar landmarks to indicate where she might be.

She grew more numb. She should eat some jerky and biscuits. She'd gone too long without food. Shelby gazed upward at the cliff down which she had fallen. It was almost perpendicular. Bruised as she was, she could never make it to the top. Her only choice was to climb down as best she could.

The wind had packed the snow. If she lay on her back and slid, maybe she could reach the bottom. She flattened herself and easily conquered the first little slope.

"It's easy!" she exclaimed and laughed aloud for one joyous moment.

Suddenly, sick with fear, she felt herself slipping out of control. She tried to dig her toes into the cliff, but it was icy and her booted feet couldn't gain a toehold. Her hands reached to grab a branch, a shrub, anything! But they came away empty.

Then, just when she was sure she was going to plunge to her death against the rocks at the bottom, Shelby rammed into a tangle of deerbrush.

She had become so stiff she could not turn herself around and crawl out. Doggedly, she began to work herself out backward, inch by inch. Her limbs had grown numb with cold, and the pain caused by the squirming motion intensified. For a moment she felt dizzy and faint.

"Easy, Shelby," she counseled herself. "Rest a minute. Then you can slide the rest of the way."

It was an extreme pleasure to stop her struggling and simply lie still.

Braden beat at the fear inside. Tried to keep it under control so he could think. Very little snow was falling now and the clouds had thinned, occasionally exposing little scraps of blue sky. The sight would have been comforting, but the wind had shifted from south to west which meant the storm wasn't done yet.

If he hurried, there would still be enough daylight for him to get to Butte Station and beyond, if necessary. He knew the trail well enough to make it to Mountain Springs Station and on to Ruby Valley. Braden assured himself he would find Shelby safe at one of these places.

Now the wind was fast turning into a gale. Unhindered, it swept across the meadow, but when Braden rode into the shelter of the canyon walls, the wind picked up the snow and drove it furiously into every crack and crevice. From the crest of the windward side of the canyon, the swirling, eddying snow looked like a white banner waving from the mountainside. *Surrender, Braden, surrender*, the whistling wind seemed to be saying.

The drifts were building so fast within the canyon walls that Braden could see them rising before his eyes. He picked his way along, permitting himself no thought beyond the next step. That Shelby might not be warm and safe in one of the Pony stations was unbearable.

He no longer felt watchful eyes as he rode, and he amused himself by imagining his foes curled in a cramped cold shelter, struggling to build a fire with hands stiff and nonfunctioning from the chill wind.

Once through the canyon and again on the desert floor, Braden found going much easier. Here the wind had blown away most of the covering of snow, though it continued to fall at a steady rate. As the wind slacked off, the visibility improved, and Braden made fine time to Butte Station.

Seeing Braden, the station tender and hostler rushed out to him. "Got the mail?" one of them shouted.

Braden felt his stomach lurch. Shelby wasn't here!

The two men offered to help with the search, but he discouraged them. If there were any clues left after the storm ended, he didn't want them obliterated by well-meaning but unskilled trackers.

"Thanks, but if the kid comes in, he'll need your help. Better that you stay here."

Having decided that Shelby had ridden straight for Ruby Valley, Braden refused to consider any alternatives. The kid wouldn't need a change of horses since he wasn't trying to make time, so that would be the wise move.

The two made no move to appeal Braden's decision, so he rode on alone.

At the crest of the butte the wind picked up, but the real problem was the snow falling thick and heavy, like feathers spilling from a down pillow, the flakes descending in an impenetrable mass. His hat lowered and his shoulders hunched against the driving snow, Braden fought to see a few steps in front of him.

He rode slowly along the rim of the butte, giving the horse plenty of rein, trusting the animal's instincts to find the best way. They started down along the east face, around a point in the trail, and into a swirling blizzard.

Unable to bear any thoughts of Shelby alone and in trouble, he concentrated instead on the storm. He never could figure any logic to the ways of drifting snow. Against a dead tree the snow always piled itself on the windward side. But at the crest of a cliff, it built out on the lee side. Farther and farther it stretched into space until the big blunt snow shelf would extend for six or eight feet, threatening to drop and bury anything passing underneath.

Then . . . he heard it! The sound was unmistakable. He kicked the pony in the ribs, and the startled beast leaped sideways.

"Come on!" Braden shouted as he fought to straighten out the horse.

The strange low hissing noise gradually grew higher in pitch and intensity. Through the falling snow Braden could see nothing. But as they ran, the whole canyon vibrated with some sudden impact.

The hissing changed to a thudding. Like an ocean in turmoil, an undulating wave of snow rolled swiftly toward them, pinning the pony and Braden astride him against the sheer rock of the canyon wall. Then it roared on past, leaving them in three feet of snow.

In the wake of the avalanche, there was a sudden hush.

Still pinned against the wall, Braden looked quickly to his left down the canyon. Some twenty feet below, the wave of snow had come to a halt. For a few moments, with massive pressure behind it, it had raged madly until it spent itself and lay in a soggy heap.

Braden dismounted to lead his horse as they floundered ahead. Once clear of the deep snow, he swung back into the saddle and continued on his way to Ruby Valley. When he came free of the canyon, he urged the pony to a brisk pace through the desert where the snow had been blown into drifts against the sagebrush and willows, leaving much of the ground clear.

He arrived at Ruby Station just as pale rays broke through the clouds. The position of the brassy sun announced the finale of its ever-lengthening arc through the southern sky. As he rode into the yard he watched it sink behind the tall peaks sheltering the station.

Uncle Billy Rogers dashed out to meet Braden. "Hello, Russell! Got the mail?"

Braden's heart stopped. He looked wildly around the corral, but there was no chestnut with a corkscrew of hair in the middle of its forehead. Only Nick Wilson, the Pony rider, was there, helping the hostler saddle a fresh pony.

Billy looked puzzled. "Expectin' someone?"

"Mail's not here yet?" Braden managed to ask.

"'Course it ain't. Nick wouldn't be here waitin' if it was." Billy looked thoroughly disgusted.

Nick walked over and took the reins of Braden's worn horse. "What's the matter, Braden?"

"We've lost a rider and the mail in the blizzard." Braden forced himself to say the words, feeling as he did that he was sealing Shelby's doom.

"Then we got to get out and find him," Billy said. "Nick, you stay here so's you'll be fresh to ride when we bring in the mail." Shouting orders at the hostler, Billy ran to the corral and led out the fresh mounts. "Ain't got an idee where the kid might have lost the trail, have ya?" Billy asked.

Braden shook his head and let his body go slack. As long as there had been hope, he had managed to keep his exhaustion at bay. Now he permitted himself to feel its full impact.

"We'd best split up," Billy ventured. "I'll ride one side of the butte. You take t'other. Whoever finds the mail, ride back to Ruby Valley with it."

Braden nodded his agreement, too worn to see the flaw in Billy's plan, whirled his pony about, and galloped away into the twilight.

Forbidding his emotions to surface, he refused to face them, preferring instead to ride blind and numb. Not until the pony slowed, lathered and winded, did Braden come to his senses and begin to think about how he would search for Shelby in a land distorted by drifts of swirling snow.

## CHAPTER 17

DESPERATE TO FIND SHELBY, Braden—dizzy and sick and tired, so tired—rode on. In his weariness, he could no longer keep from thinking.

Accusations rose thick and fast, galling Braden until he nearly choked. If he hadn't been so obsessed with tracking Jane Ann's killers, he would have been at Egan Station to take the mail. The kid would be safe and so would the mail. Blinding hatred rose in great waves to wash over him, but this time the hate wasn't for those responsible for his sister's death. It was directed at himself.

His mind drifted back to the conversation Shelby and he had had in the reading room at the Ormsby House. He could see the intense look on Shelby's face and hear the kid's words. "Vengeance is the Lord's and punishment for such crimes is for the law. When you begin meting out your own justice, you become no better than those who committed the original acts."

"No! That's not true!" he roared. But something inside bore witness to the fact, and he couldn't will the feeling away. It shrouded him, weighing him down until his head hung but inches from the saddle horn.

Finally Braden could stand it no longer. He straightened in the saddle and threw back his head. "Oh, God!" he shouted his anger into the fierce wind. "Show me why! Why the people I love most are taken from me?" Sobs wracked his body and tears froze on his cheeks. "Nobody's doing anything about Jane Ann's murder but me. I can't let the butchers who killed her go unpunished!"

Braden rode slowly now, letting Will's story of Jane Ann's death roll through his head. If Will had told it right, he had to face the fact that her killing hadn't been planned. Innocent of the plot, she had unwittingly gotten in the way. "But, God, nobody has a right to kill an innocent person. Not for any reason."

*And nobody outside the law has a right to kill somebody for any reason,* he heard from deep inside.

"All right, I'll make a bargain," Braden replied. "I'll give up hunting Jane Ann's killers if you'll help me find Shelby."

This time his words were greeted by a deep silence, weighted and cold.

He journeyed on without seeing, letting the wind tear at him, unwind the red muffler from his face and whip it like a flag—the muffler Shelby had given him for his birthday. *Funny the kid would remember my birthday. Only mentioned it once.* Though unable to stop the memories of the times the two of them had spent together, he was unable to think of a single genuinely unpleasant moment. Oh, there had been times he'd had to admonish the boy, but always there was instant contrition in the green eyes and a willing spirit.

At last the hurting became too much to bear. If he ceased pondering, he reasoned, his brain would become numb; ceased feeling, and his heart would turn to blue ice, and with each beat a small chip would shave off and vanish. In a short time his heart would disappear altogether, and he would never have to feel again. Thinking would then no longer cause pain, and he could stand to go on living.

But the pain inside did not diminish. Rather, it strengthened until it tore through him with a searing heat despite the frigid temperature.

"It's not fair!" he shouted in Shelby's defense. "The kid's never had a break. He ought to have a chance to live. To grow up. He's a good little guy. The best I ever knew." Angry tears squeezed out of eyes squinted against the glare. "I offered to bargain. What about it?"

*Is having Shelby worth giving up your revenge? Worth returning to God? No bargains, Braden.*

Braden gave a harsh laugh. "And you'll take care of the punishment, I suppose! You'll see that those two scalawags receive justice enough to satisfy me!" Braden's contemptuous voice rolled into the wind.

*Do not mock me! Vengeance is mine!*

The voice resounded through Braden, leaving him weak and trembling. The vindictiveness around which he had built his life for nearly a year crumbled in the face of such force. But a black unfeeling void opened where his hate had been, drawing him, helpless and spent, into the chasm.

Time stopped as though held in suspension. Braden felt no future, only eons of this moment, the now a promise of his eternity. The void began slowly swallowing him, covering him over, and capturing his soul in its unending emptiness.

Terror constricted his throat and banded his eyes. This vast nothingness was worse than the hate. He couldn't live like this.

Slowly he slid from his saddle and knelt on the snow-covered trail.

Taking a deep breath, he began, "Oh, God, I'm at the end of myself. I don't know where to go from here. Haven't called your name for too long, but I'm begging now. I'm here to ask you to forgive the mess I've made of things."

At Braden's acknowledgment of God, the wind took on a life of its own. It flicked snow in his face, taunted him with sharp gusts, toyed with him in the eye of a tiny cyclone.

"Please, Lord, help me." Braden was nearly drowning in anguish.

The wind picked up the pace of its fight with Braden. It

flew at him, loud and shrill. Then, filling its lungs, it spewed an icy blast down the canyon. It drove the snow in blinding waves before it, threatening to freeze the unprotected man and beast in its wake.

Braden, understanding his very existence was being challenged, continued, "Let me back into your light and love," he implored.

Angered by Braden's stubborn resistance and determined to bring about his destruction, the Devil-wind raged at the kneeling man like a mad thing, screaming past him, tearing at him. He snatched the muffler, and the wind flung it away, leaving a long red scar bleeding on the snow.

And still Braden prayed. "Cleanse my heart of wickedness and purify my thoughts," he pleaded with his rediscovered Lord.

Furious, the wind roared like a deadly beast locked in mortal combat. It clawed at Braden with ice crystals sharp enough to draw blood. Sucked the air away before he could breath it, leaving him gasping. Drove the cold into the marrow of his bones. Froze his extremities until they were leaden weights.

Crouching lower into the protection of his arms, Braden promised, "Thy will be done, O Lord God. Thy will be done." He concluded in a whisper, and sinking back onto his heels, raised his arms heavenward and gave himself, heart, mind, and soul to his Master.

There issued from the screeching wind such a blast as Braden had never before experienced. He felt his body being lifted toward the edge of the cliff, with nothing to grasp, nothing to hinder his fall.

"Lord!" Braden cried as he prepared to meet his Maker. "Please take care of Shelby!"

The wind contorted, twisted, lost its direction and strength. It moaned pitifully as it clung to the canyon walls, swirling in patternless impotency. It sobbed a feeble cry as it attempted to regain its former power. Drew on its reserve strength and spent it on one last frigid blast.

Braden breathed in life, renewed his strength, felt it fill him, arm him.

The wind sighed its defeat, yet did not give up graciously. Rather, it groveled in an ineffectual puff and died, leaving a moment of total silence at its passing.

Braden dragged himself from his knees and into the saddle. With head bowed and eyes closed, he rode. The stone in his breast gradually dissolved and though he had been with little sleep or food for twenty-four hours, he felt renewed and warm inside.

"Praise the Lord," he whispered. "Praise the Lord!" The shout rang out, light and free, filling the canyon. His spirit drank in the words, hope returned, and he traveled in a stream of light. The glory of the Lord shone round about Braden and healed him. Made him warm and secure even in the face of the terrible blizzard.

Then, without warning, the horse shied, pitching Braden against the canyon wall. Its terrified scream filled the silence, and a tipsy sidestep nearly unseated the unsuspecting rider.

He leaped from the saddle, his gun drawn, and eased along the unfamiliar route lighted only by a cloud-streaked moon. Pulling the quivering pony behind him, Braden moved slowly up the trail. Again, the horse reared and whinnied.

"What's the matter, boy?" he asked, knowing that these well-trained ponies didn't spook easily.

Then, Braden's foot struck something. Two large lumps covered with snow protruded from the rock wall and into the trail. There was a familiarity about their shapes that made Braden uneasy.

Slowly he reached down and brushed the snow off a gun barrel. He shook his head and sighed. There, frozen fingers clasping the gun barrel aimed down the trail, lay Will, his face still tight and unforgiving. Huddled next to Will for warmth and looking as if he had just gone to sleep was Elwood P. Hawker. Braden bowed his head and said a prayer for the two conspirators.

Strange. Now that they were dead, he felt no joy. Instead, he felt sorrow that they had led such loveless lives and died for so small and selfish a cause—trying to keep the riches of California for themselves.

"Thank you, Lord, for rescuing me from such an end."

The trail was extremely narrow here, and there was no convincing the half-wild pony to step that close to the dead men. Braden was forced to turn around. He would bring horses and men and come back when it was light.

As he walked the pony down the canyon trail, he became aware that the air had stilled. The clouds moved over the surface of the moon and disappeared, leaving pure unfiltered moonlight shining through the darkness.

Head bowed, Braden prayed for Shelby's safety. With the clearing of the clouds, the temperature would begin to plummet. He must find the kid soon.

A weak nicker from off the trail broke into Braden's thoughts. His pony gave an answering whinny. Braden looked over the edge of a precipice. It was a sheer drop to the next outcropping of rock on which lay large snow-covered lumps. From there was another steep descent into the bottom of the canyon.

Suddenly there was a movement.

Braden let out a Paiute war cry, the only thing violent enough to release his pent-up emotions.

Feeling carefully, he found the end of the rock wall and moved off the trail and down the mountain as rapidly as its icy decline would allow. The pony nickered a weak welcome. After brushing off the snow, Braden recognized Corkscrew, pinned between two large rocks. With trembling hands, he removed the mochila and saddle, and by working the pony's head around was able to get the animal on its feet.

Braden ran a practiced hand over the pony. Miraculously, though he had a few cuts, there seemed to be no broken bones.

"All right, boy," Braden spoke softly to the frightened animal, "where's Shelby?"

Leaving Corkscrew, Braden quickly searched among the other heaps of snow. Nothing gave a hint of Shelby's whereabouts, and panic pulsed in him. Sick at heart, Braden sank onto a rock, letting his body go slack.

Coyotes howling in the bottom of the canyon interrupted his brooding. Braden walked to the rim of the rock and looked down. Below, the dark shapes circled something lying in the snow.

"No!" he shouted. After pulling the revolver from his holster, he fired a shot into the air to frighten the animals away.

Racing down the slope as fast as he dared, he was soon standing over the unconscious figure. He hadn't the courage to learn if Shelby was dead or alive. He gathered the limp little body in his arms and slipped and slid his way up the mountain, praying fervently as he climbed.

Shelby gradually became aware of a terrible ache in her side and almost unbearable stabbing pains shooting from her hands and feet. She opened her eyes and looked about. A blanket was suspended over a wire stretched from one wall of the cabin to the other, affording her some privacy. Strange. Privacy was something she had learned to live without.

She lay still a moment, savoring the quiet and the warmth. She didn't know when she had felt so warm. Even through the haze of pain, she could recall having been so cold, so very cold. She was safe now. Someone had found her, rescued her, and she closed her eyes to thank God for sparing her life. But who? And how had it come about?

While lifting an arm to pull the quilt under her chin, she paused in midair to regard it, covered with a pink flannel sleeve, ruffled at the wrist. Peering under the covers, she found another ruffle at the hem of the long nightgown. Aunt Ruby knew!

Panic filled Shelby. Aunt Ruby would surely tell, and Bolivar Roberts would as surely dismiss her. What would she do? She would never be able to find another job that paid nearly what she was earning now. Besides, she liked taking care of the animals, liked the wild country, liked her life. She didn't want to go back to St. Joe.

At last she allowed herself to focus on the real reason for her panic. She couldn't bear facing what Braden would do when he found out. A tear slipped down her cheek. Though her entire body ached, it was nothing compared to the ache in her heart at the thought of never seeing him again.

The slight chink of spurs told Shelby someone was coming across the room toward her bed. She sat up quickly, combed her hair with her fingers, and spread the covers neatly around herself. Smiling as wide and bright a smile as she could muster, she turned to see a hand draw the blanket aside. Her breath caught. Braden!

She met his cool gaze as it studied her, and the smile congealed as she felt the blood leave her face. Her hands flew like startled birds to her throat, and nervously, she fingered the creamy lace ruffle that accented the feminine gown. Her mouth turned dry, and when she tried to speak, no words would come. She licked her lips with little flicks of an also dry tongue, staring in stunned silence at Braden, his taut body drawn to its full height, granite-hard eyes glaring at her from a shuttered face.

Then, no match for his strength, she shrank against the wall, cowering before him, waiting his first words with anxious flutterings in her stomach.

"Well, kid," he said in a frigid voice. "It's nice to see you're finally awake." But he didn't sound glad at all, not even slightly. He moved in behind the concealing blanket, sat on the edge of her cot, and fingered the lace at her wrist. "Pretty fancy night clothes for a boy."

Didn't he know? Surely, he must. The flutterings tightened into knots in her stomach. She looked for some sign of acceptance, but he sat rigid, not even the tiniest light of compassion flickered over his stern, handsome face.

"Au—Aunt Ruby didn't tell you?" Shelby stammered, her voice quivering, her heart contracting with the coldness of his reception. How could she tell him? With a sinking feeling, she knew that she had to tell him her story, and when she did, she would lose him forever.

He looked at her with a quizzical eye. "Aunt Ruby didn't tell me what?

Shelby straightened her shoulders, though the pain

made the act difficult, and ruthlessly pushed aside all emotion. "I'm not a boy."

"Prove it!" He stared at her in unblinking hostility.

She smothered a small gasp. *You can't mean that*, she thought as tears sprang to her eyes. But he sat in statuelike rigidity, giving her no quarter. Her throat ached with choked-back sobs as she picked nervously at the quilt.

At last recovering slightly from the shock of his request, she found her voice and said in a hoarse whisper, "You don't really want me to prove to you that I am not a boy."

"And if I do?"

"Then you're not the man I thought you were."

He regarded her a while longer before he spoke, the glacial cold still radiating from his grim face. When he spoke however, his voice, warm and gentle, destroyed the hostile mood. "Of course I wouldn't ask you to prove anything, but I thought you should suffer just a bit for what you put me through. That was a rotten trick to play, Shelby. Really rotten." With the stone facade softened, his intense weariness showed in cheekbones standing out in stark relief against the sharp ridges under his gray velvet eyes.

"I'm sorry, Braden," she whispered. "I truly am." Though she wanted to pour out her love for him, cry, threaten, beg, she found herself curiously quiet. "I didn't know what else to do. How else to earn a respectable living. I never meant to take advantage of you or your protection." She looked deeply into Braden's eyes and watched his containment crack, as an ice jam cracks under the spring sun.

He chuckled deep in his throat. "Poor Ruby let out a shriek that made the Paiute war cry sound sickly."

She sat transfixed, unbelieving. "You knew all the time! And you let me make a fool of myself!" A deep flush rose from her neck, filling her face, and her lips trembled with building anger.

"I needed some time to sort things out," Braden said in a matter-of-fact voice. "That was quite a discovery to swallow all at once. Also, I wanted to see if you'd confess on your own." He picked up her hand.

"What are you holding my hand for? Planning to break my fingers, one by one?" She made her voice cold and cutting. She had to hide her feelings behind something.

"The thought had occurred to me, but then I decided that wasn't painful enough to pay you back for making me out such a fool." His voice remained warm, gentle in its teasing, and his eyes glowed with tenderness as he studied her face.

This tender, caring Braden was unfamiliar. She didn't know him, but the prospect of becoming acquainted intrigued her.

"I didn't know what else to do, Braden. Papa warned me about being a lone woman in this country."

"And Papa was right." He ran his fingertips over her forehead and brushed back some wayward locks of hair. "Tell me, was your hair long before you cut it?"

She nodded. "Nearly to my waist."

He paled. Confusion shattered his features. He studied her face intently. "Did you own a flowered calico dress?"

Relieved at the trivial question, she laughed. "Every pioneer woman owns such a dress."

His eyes narrowed, and he gazed at her as if trying to see through her.

"Braden," Shelby whispered. "What is it?"

"The cabin you lived in with your father. Tell me about it."

"You mean inside?"

"I mean everything."

She clasped her hands and for the first time since she left, she pictured the desolate little shack and described it to him, from the checkered cloth she had brought to brighten up the dismal inside to the watering trough in the corral that captured a small spring of water.

Braden turned gray as a ghost and passed a hand over his forehead. Though his throat worked, no words came forth.

His looks frightened her. "Braden, what's the matter?" she cried.

He sat for a long time in silent contemplation, only the crackling of the fire and the ceaseless ticking of the clock breaking the quiet. At last color returned to his face, and Braden cleared his throat. "What I am about to tell you, I have never shared with anyone."

When he finished the story of his dream, he asked, "Will you grow it that way again? For me?"

Shelby's heart faltered as she nodded. What was he suggesting? She felt suddenly shy, and she dropped her eyes, their dark fringe feathering her cheeks.

Braden's heart gave a lurch. In these past few hours, everything had come clear. Why he'd longed to protect him—*her*. Why he never wanted to leave her side again.

He cleared his throat of the catch that threatened to take his breath away. "Uh, Shelby your real name?"

"Yes," she said, lifting those marvelous eyes to his. "I was supposed to be a boy, and Papa already had my name picked out. Just couldn't seem to call me anything else, so it stuck."

"It suits you." He continued to hold her hand. "I have more things to tell you. Are you well enough to hear them?"

"Of course. I'm not sick, just battered. By the way, whom do I have to thank for saving my life? I don't remember much after I fell."

Braden let his eyes linger on her face. "I found you," he said simply. Then, still rubbing her fingers, he told her the story of her rescue.

She waited until he was finished to ask about Will. "I suspected Elwood P. Hawker of something illegal, but Will? He seemed so nice."

"He fooled me, too. But when I began checking into the stages that were robbed, I learned he was the driver on all of them. I also discovered the 'Knights,' as they call themselves, wanted to make our ranch their headquarters and the capitol of their new Pacific Coast country. They tried to buy the ranch, but we wouldn't sell. By taking our money and plundering the freight wagons, they hoped to ruin us and force us out.

"The Pony kept everyone in the East informed of

'Knights' activities out here, so it was important to stop the Pony from running. Will was one of the head men. Hawker was under him. Interesting how it all worked out."

Shelby was fascinated by Braden's story, but what had happened to the bitter, vengeful man she had traveled so many miles with? "I don't understand your acceptance of all this. There's more you're not telling me."

A shy smile spread over Braden's face and this time reached his eyes, making them sparkle. "You're right. There is more and you had considerable to do with it." Though emotion clouded his voice and tears glistened in his eyes, Braden managed to tell Shelby the story of his repentance and the Lord's forgiveness.

When he finished, Shelby tried to speak over the huge lump in her throat, but instead, brushed away her tears and reached to touch his cheek.

The silence between them grew, but it was a comfortable silence, and Braden's touch took away the pain that had wakened her. Gradually she relaxed into a deep, healing sleep.

Shelby roused occasionally, but each time, Braden or Ruby was there with her. The next time she awoke fully, the darkened room was tinted with the rosy glow of firelight.

There, stretched in front of the fire was Braden, sleeping peacefully. His face, relaxed for the first time since she had known him, reflected a tranquility she had never imagined there. *Thank you, Lord, for making him well.*

He stirred as though feeling her gaze and rolled over. Their eyes locked and held. Then he smiled, raised up, and came to her, taking her carefully into his arms.

"My darling Shelby," he whispered. "How are you feeling?"

"Better, now." She snuggled against him. "Have I been sick long?"

"Five days."

"Five days! That can't be."

"That was a terrible ordeal you suffered through. You've been getting steadily better, though. Ruby says you're going to be up and about in no time."

"And then what will I do? Once Mr. Roberts finds out I'm not a boy, he'll fire me for sure."

"I don't anticipate any problems. I'd like to think you're ready to give up working for the Pony and settle down to being a beloved wife and mother."

"But . . . But you hardly know me . . . at least not as a girl. Are you sure you want *me*? Not Miss Lila . . . or maybe someday, Mrs. Ormsby . . . or . . . ?

"Hush Shelby. It's *you* I love, have loved from the moment I saw you standing by the trail last spring, looking more pitiful and woebegone than anything I can ever remember."

Shelby wrapped her arms around his neck, and he pulled her tightly against his broad chest. "Then its time I confessed something. I've loved you too, for nearly that long. It's made pretending to be a boy simply awful!"

He chuckled. "Think how I've felt, thinking you *were* one! I was about ready to adopt you!" Then, his mood grew reflective as he studied her upturned face. "As I look at you now, it is incredible to me that I didn't recognize you as the love of my dream. How could I possibly have missed it?"

She slipped her arms away and sat back, looking deep into luminous eyes filled with the intensity of his love for her. "It was not in the Lord's time. There was much we both needed to resolve in our lives, ghosts to lay to rest. Now, our pasts are behind us. Sharp grief has turned to sweet memories, and we are free to love, to share fully our lives with one another."

He kissed her lips, and Shelby felt herself drawn to him, felt the last cold spot in her heart dissolve and fill with the warmth of his love.

After long moments Braden exhaled a deep sigh and held Shelby from him, studying her for a prolonged moment. Then, in the gruff voice she had come to know so well, he asked, "Well, kid, you ready to travel?" A slow grin tipped his mouth. "We've got a long life ahead of us, and I'd like to get on with sharing it."

Visions of them riding alone as they had once done flashed through her mind. "Braden!"

His mouth twitched with amusement as he read her thoughts. "Supply wagon's due. Driver can chaperone us until we get to Carson City. There we can make everything legal. That suit you?"

Her face filled with a radiating glow, and she nodded. "Just one thing, more. Please stop calling me 'kid'," she pleaded.

Throwing back his head, he laughed uproariously. Then sobering, he took her small tapering hand in his strong one. "Shelby, I've loved you so long by that name, I'm not sure I can. Does it really bother you that much?"

"No, but won't people think it strange—referring to your wife in such terms?"

Lights danced in his eyes, giving the gray a satin sheen. "Probably, but then everything about us is out of the ordinary."

Shelby snuggled against him again, letting love and contentment bind them together. She was home, at last.

## ABOUT THE AUTHOR

So full of fancy and tall tales is MARYN LANGER that one would never suspect that she spends her days teaching mathematics to junior high students, nor that she has written textbooks in her chosen field. Although she loves teaching, she looks forward to retiring and devoting herself to full-time writing.

While researching for *Ride with Wings*, Langer contacted the Pony Express Association and was invited to participate in the 125th reride of the Pony during the summer of 1985.

The author lives with her husband in what she describes as "a teacup of a mountain valley in southcentral Idaho." Their tiny town (under 300 people) is completely surrounded by mountains.

*Forever Classics* are inspirational romances designed to bring you a joyful, heart-lifting reading experience. If you would like more information about joining our *Forever Classics* book series, please write to us:

>Guideposts Customer Service
>39 Seminary Hill Road
>Carmel, NY 10512

*Forever Classics* are chosen by the same staff that prepares *Guideposts*, a monthly magazine filled with true stories of people's adventures in faith. *Guideposts* is not sold on the newsstand. It's available by subscription only. And subscribing is easy. Write to the address above and you can begin reading *Guideposts* soon. When you subscribe, each month you can count on receiving exciting new evidence of God's Presence, His Guidance and His limitless love for all of us.